MENAGE A MAGICK

USA Today Bestselling Author

LORA LEIGH

ELLORA'S CAVE
ROMANTICA PUBLISHING

An Ellora's Cave Romantica Publication

www.ellorascave.com

Menage A Magick

ISBN 1843606186, 9781843606185
ALL RIGHTS RESERVED.
Menage A Magick Copyright © 2003 Lora Leigh
Cover art by Scott Carpenter

Trade paperback Publication 2003

Content Advisory:

S – ENSUOUS
E – ROTIC
X – TREME

Ellora's Cave Publishing offers three levels of Romantica™ reading entertainment: S (S-ensuous), E (E-rotic), and X (X-treme).

The following material contains graphic sexual content meant for mature readers. This story has been rated E–rotic.

S-*ensuous* love scenes are explicit and leave nothing to the imagination.

E-*rotic* love scenes are explicit, leave nothing to the imagination, and are high in volume per the overall word count. E-rated titles might contain material that some readers find objectionable — in other words, almost anything goes, sexually. E-rated titles are the most graphic titles we carry in terms of both sexual language and descriptiveness in these works of literature.

X-*treme* titles differ from E-rated titles only in plot premise and storyline execution. Stories designated with the letter X tend to contain difficult or controversial subject matter not for the faint of heart.

Also by Lora Leigh

৯০

A Wish, A Kiss, A Dream *(anthology)*

B.O.B.'s Fall (with Veronica Chadwick)

Bound Hearts 1: Surrender

Bound Hearts 2: Submission

Bound Hearts 3: Seduction

Bound Hearts 4: Wicked Intent

Bound Hearts 5: Sacrifice

Bound Hearts 6: Embraced

Bound Hearts 7: Shameless

Cowboy & the Captive

Coyote Breeds 1: Soul Deep

Elemental Desires *(anthology)*

Feline Breeds 1: Tempting the Beast

Feline Breeds 2: The Man Within

Feline Breeds 3: Kiss of Heat

Law and Disorder 1: Moving Violations (with Veronica Chadwick)

Manaconda *(anthology)*

Men of August 1: Marly's Choice

Men of August 2: Sarah's Seduction

Men of August 3: Heather's Gift

Men of August 4: August Heat (12 Quickies of Christmas)

Wizard Twins 2: When Wizards Rule

Wolf Breeds 1: Wolfe's Hope

Wolf Breeds 2: Jacob's Faith

Wolf Breeds 3: Aiden's Charity

Wolf Breeds 4: Elizabeth's Wolf

About the Author

୨୦

Lora Leigh is a wife and mother living in Kentucky. She dreams in bright, vivid images of the characters intent on taking over her writing life, and fights a constant battle to put them on the hard drive of her computer before they can disappear as fast as they appeared.

Lora's family, and her writing life co-exist, if not in harmony, in relative peace with each other. An understanding husband is the key to late nights with difficult scenes, and stubborn characters. His insights into human nature, and the workings of the male psyche provide her hours of laughter, and innumerable romantic ideas that she works tirelessly to put into effect.

Lora Leigh welcomes comments from readers. You can find her website and email address on her author bio page at www.ellorascave.com.

MENAGE A MAGICK

Dedication

ೞ

To the League Of Needy Readers (LONR):

May you forever have a warm fire, hot chocolate and plenty of your favorite books for your heart's desire.

Warmest regards, Lora Leigh

Chapter One

ଙ

The soft glow from the aura of magick that surrounded the twin moons of Sentmar was slowly dissipating. The twin rings were thinner than they had been in the entire written history of the planet. Once, thick luminous rings surrounded the moons, like pillowy circles of thick, rich cream. They were now wispy, and more transparent than ever before.

The magick of the land was growing weaker by the year now, instead of by the decade. They would have to move quickly, or it would be too late. The humans would once again rule the land and they would have no mercy for their magick counterparts.

Lasan stood on the upper balcony of the Veraga castle and stared into the night sky, frowning as he observed the phenomena. All that was Sentmar and magick was now threatened. All that had balanced justice and peace within their world was at stake.

"We must move quickly." Drago, his twin, stood behind him, staring at the moons as well, his voice soft, concerned. "She will not see reason, Lasan. Not until after the Joining. We can no longer afford to hesitate."

He was growing impatient. Lasan could feel it beating at his brain, his twin's impatience. It saddened him, concerned him. Drago, for all his stubborn disposition and determination, was rarely impatient. Lasan's natural patience had always served to stem the stubborn streak that ran through his brother.

He pushed his fingers wearily through his hair, then clasped the balustrade with an iron grip.

"We will contact Queen Amoria on the morrow," he decided. "As you say, we can wait no longer."

Queen Amoria, ruler of the house of Sellane, the ruling family of the Covenani, the sect of sorceresses that had separated themselves hundreds of years ago from the Wizards destined to complete them. Without her aid, they would be unable to approach the Princess Brianna in any manner.

Lasan had never completely understood the separation. Time had hidden the answers to his questions, and the Wizard Sentinels were silent when he came to them with his need for answers. All he and Drago knew was that they were to fix the separation. It was now their destiny, the responsibility of their world rested on their shoulders alone.

To preserve all they held dear, the woman they would have wooed to their hearts would have to be forced to their bed. It was a bitter thought to swallow. The one woman created to complete them, to bind them forever within a ring of magick, pleasure and satisfaction, had denied them.

Contemptuously, sneeringly, she had thrown their offer of Joining back in their faces, denying any link they could have shared. She was their natural Consort, and yet she ran from them at every chance.

But wasn't that what the Covenani were good at, Drago snapped within his mind. *They ran from our ancestors as this one now runs from us. Mocking the bonds between us, and her own needs.*

And this was so. They could feel the arousal that pulsed in her body when last they had touched her. Holding her between them, the heat of her body, the magick rising inside her, tormenting them with a level of lust they had never known before.

As Lasan had caressed her soft lips, Drago had smoothed his lips over her satin shoulders, exploring the softness of her flesh, warming her between them, allowing her to feel the pleasure that rose from each touch.

She had shivered in their arms, whimpered as her mouth opened, accepting a deeper kiss, a firmer caress. They had been inflamed by her response, the magick soaring through their bodies, rising, building to an aura that would have encompassed them all, forging the bond to come.

It had been then that Brianna had broken away from them. Gasping for air, shock rounding her violet eyes, her own power glittering in the dark orbs as she faced them furiously.

"Dwell on this no longer," Drago bit out from behind him. "She will come to us, Lasan. We will give her no other choice."

Lasan sighed deeply. "But perhaps it is a choice she needs to make," he murmured. "For all our future happiness."

"It is the Joining that is required, not her happiness," his brother growled.

Lasan was well aware that Drago regretted this as much as he did. They had given her every opportunity to make the choice for herself. They had all but gone to their knees in supplication. It rankled at their pride.

"Begin preparations," Lasan sighed.

They would need several sets of Wizard Twins to accompany them, as well as the Sentinel Guards, the magickal warriors who kept a tight rein on the darkness that would have invaded their lands.

"She is ours, Lasan," Drago growled. "I do not completely understand your hesitancy in this. She will come to accept us."

Lasan turned and stared at his brother. The night breeze whipped the long black hair back from his face, revealing the strong, determined lines of his expression. His eyes were a dark, emerald green, piercing and brilliant. His cheekbones high, his jaw squared and tight with his anger.

Lasan shook his head. Self-mockery filled him. He knew well that Drago's anger stemmed from his own reluctance to force this alliance. His anger that she had denied them, despite her needs, despite the knowledge that filled her, that she did indeed desire them.

Despite their powers, the advanced degree of magick that filled them, they could not break through her reserve, they could not ease whatever fears filled her enough to allow her to accept them.

"The Seculars are gaining in strength, and the dark force propelling them is gaining ground. We cannot afford even the time we have allowed her thus far," Drago reminded him. "I have called the Sashtain Twins, as well as the Alessi. They must begin to press their suits quickly if this is to succeed."

Lasan nodded firmly. "We will begin preparations to leave then. The Covenani Ball begins in two moon cycles. Ensure a fair number of Twin sets are in attendance. Cauldaran and Covenani can be separated no longer."

A millennia apart, and still the female sect of magick keepers had not returned to their male counterparts, nor expressed a desire in reaching concessions. Queen Amoria would have to see the dangers in this, whether she wanted to or not.

He knew the woman to be a good ruler, a woman said to have her people's welfare at heart. As a Queen, she was more respected than any of her predecessors. But she was still a Sorceress, and possibly determined to continue the separation out of pride and fear of the unknown.

Lasan cursed silently as he turned and stared back at the brilliant glow of the moons. The peace that the land had enjoyed for so many thousands of years could now come to an end if they did not move quickly. He closed his eyes, thinking of Brianna, her warmth, her passion. He sent his touch out to her, a most difficult maneuver considering the distance that separated them. He felt Drago's power join with his, despite the other duties he carried out.

A smile tipped Lasan's lips as he felt her sleepy response, heard her moan of passion. *Enjoy,* he whispered silently. *We come for you soon, Brianna, soon beloved, and you will know our touch in truth, as well as in dreams.*

* * * * *

"…you will know our touch in truth, as well as in dreams…" Brianna heard the whispered words as hands traveled sensually over her nude body.

Her nipples beaded as she moaned against the feel of a heated mouth enveloping them, a ghostly lick had her arching closer to the touch. Her hands clenched into the blankets, her thighs tightening, pressing together as she felt a peculiar caress between them. Gods. She tossed restlessly as phantom hands parted the lips of her sex, and a moist, liquid swipe of a patient tongue ran through the heated slit, then circled the throbbing, aching bud of her clit. Sensation gathered within her, pulling at her, drawing her deeper into pleasure, closer to paradise.

She was awash in heated need. She pressed her breasts closer to the warmth of male hands, knowing the danger, knowing even in sleep that it was Drago's lips feeding voraciously at her nipples, and Lasan's tongue, patient and sure, that lapped at the slick moisture between her thighs.

Even in sleep, beneath the spell of their magick touch, she knew the differences. Knew who touched where, whose magick warmed her breasts, and whose lips suckled at her throbbing clit. Whose fingers were sliding tentatively, gently into...

"Wake up! Wake up, Princess! Their evil is infecting you. Sly, merciless bastards. Wake up now, I say!" A vicious pinch on her tender arm and the coarse, fearful voice of her old nurse had Brianna jerking awake.

Fear washed over her. Brilliant blue and green coils of magick wrapped around her body. They were beautiful. So velvety soft as they caressed her, filled her with warmth and desire. She felt adored...

"Trickery. Evil is what they beget," Elspeth snarled as she pinched Brianna again, her expression filled with terror. "Block them, Princess. Stop them now before they tear you apart with their magick alone."

As the nurse ranted, she felt a warmth probing with soft insistence at her vagina. She shuddered in pleasure, her body wracked by heat and need. She could feel a pressure building, an uncontrollable surge of such sensation she nearly cried aloud. Her eyes widening, Brianna fought the blankets that twisted around her body as well. She cried out in fear as she felt that warmth, a magick caress, a tender probing at the tightly closed bud of her anus.

She fought desperately for the words that would block the Wizards so daring as to send their touch across the distance that separated her. Her hands reached out to draw the magick that lived in the very air she breathed. She called on the Sorceress Matriarch, on the divinely female goddess who would protect her. As weak as even her fledgling power was, it was enough to allow her to break free of their hold and to jump from the bed.

She watched, almost with regret, as the magick coils slowly dissipated, then disappeared, once again a part of the land and the air around her.

"They are strong." She trembled, turning to Elspeth as she twisted her hands together worriedly. "They weren't cruel, Elspeth…"

"Do you think I lie?" Elspeth's voice was harsh, furious. Her expression was drawn into pinched ·lines of hatred as she faced Brianna. "Would I lie about my own child? How I held her, broken and bleeding to her death, a victim of their foul magick?"

Brianna shook her head desperately. She remembered Elspeth's daughter, once a playmate to herself and her sisters. The small, shy girl had possessed an endearing grin, but a shadow of fear always darkened her eyes. She seemed wary around her mother, though Elspeth has always been kind and gentle to Brianna and her sisters. The girl's death had been terribly upsetting to Brianna and the house of Sellane. The brutal rape was laid at the door of Wizard Twins, though there was no proof to be found that any had traveled to the lands of the Covenani.

"No, Elspeth, you wouldn't lie," she whispered, but she wondered. A small warning ember of suspicion flared inside her. "I will go sleep with Marina tonight," she continued, breathing harshly. "They cannot find me there, that close to Mother."

Elspeth took a deep, hard breath. Her wrinkled features were slowly easing, the fanatic, hard gleam in her eyes softening. She nodded her graying head firmly.

"You will do this. Go to your mother, tell her that the bastards assault you in your own bed," Elspeth ordered. "The monsters think to force an alliance with you. To destroy your innocent body. I will protect you from this, my Princess. No matter the cost, I will protect you."

Brianna backed away from the sudden flame of fury that flared once again in the aging woman's pale eyes. Elspeth watched her slyly, carefully. Brianna grabbed her robe and, leaving her slippers, rushed from the bedroom.

Her body still hummed with arousal, and she could still feel the faint touch of the Twins' magick even now, despite the spell of protection. The Sorceress Matriarch was pledged to protect her from dark evil. She was Covenani. If the Veraga Twins were such monsters, why did she still feel their touch, soothing now, comforting?

She could feel their bodies like a phantom presence, tall, broad and muscular, pressed against her. They were truly gifted with a physique that would turn any woman's eye. They stood shoulders and head above her, their large frames nearly dwarfing her. Wide shoulders and taut abdomens, strong, powerful legs. The thought of their legs had her shivering with arousal and fear. She remembered well the thick growth between those legs last year, during her mother's visit to the Cauldaran lands.

They had pressed against her, their cocks so hard, so hot, they seared her skin through the clothing that separated them. Her breathing escalated further. Gods, they should not excite her so. They were monsters. Creatures without caring. And now they invaded her dreams, her sleep, using her body, her female needs against her. They would destroy her, just as they had destroyed Elspeth's daughter.

She shuddered in fear and rushed for the safety of her mother's rooms. As Queen, her powers were much stronger, her protective shields thicker. Surely her mother would heed her pleas now, and no longer allow the courtship the Veraga Twins were pressing. Surely now, her mother would see the dangers. She had to.

Chapter Two

ᔐ

"I have given the Veraga Twins official leave to declare their suit for Consortship with you, Brianna. They will arrive soon, to allow you time to better come to know them, before the declaration is presented."

The next afternoon, Brianna stood disbelieving before her mother and her oldest sister, Serena, within the sitting room of the Queen. Not just her mother. When you were called to the official sitting room, you faced Queen Amoria, not Mother.

"You can't mean this," she whispered faintly, feeling an alarming weakness that nearly brought her to her knees. "Mother, please. They assaulted me. How can you reward them in such a way?"

She was nearing hysteria. She had never imagined that confiding to her mother the night before would bring such consequences. How could this be happening? All she had asked for was protection against their harassment, their touch when she was asleep and vulnerable to their magick. Was this too much to ask of her Queen, who was also her mother?

"Brianna, I am not ordering you into this Joining," Queen Amoria said softly. Not Mother. Mother would never do such a thing, Brianna agonized. "I am merely giving them my consent to court you. The decision ultimately rests with you."

Brianna shook her head. Her mother's expression was concerned, her golden eyes dark with worry. How could she make such a decision?

"I do not understand this." She clasped her hands before her to still their shaking as she gazed at the Queen, imploring. "I have told you numerous times, I will not accept their deviant suit. This is not what I wish."

Queen Amoria took a deep, controlled breath.

"This castle, Brianna, is not without its safeguards. Never is it undefended from unwanted magick. I do not know what your conscious mind believes, but the Veraga Wizards could not have reached out to you, within your own bed, beneath my protection, did you not somehow trust in them." Her voice was crisp, firm.

Brianna trembled beneath her steady regard as she shook her head desperately.

"It is trickery," she whispered. "You know the tales…"

"Unfounded gossip, Brianna. I have told you this often," Queen Amoria chastised her. "The Wizards are many things, but rapists and destroyers of children, they are not.

"I deny their suit." Brianna refused to address the Queen's words. She stared at the wall over the dark auburn head of her Queen mother, fighting the fury and the fear rising inside her.

Silence ascended the sitting room for long moments. Into the tense atmosphere came a soft, mocking sound of leathery hands clapping.

"Wonderful performance, Princess," Garron, her instructor, and known to be the last surviving dragon of magick, materialized within the room.

He wasn't a massive dragon, perhaps eight feet in height, his large wings folded precisely on his back, his head tilted arrogantly as Brianna met his mocking gaze furiously. She flushed, remembering her last lesson under his tutelage, where he had caught her going through the pictures in the Forbidden books. Books on sexuality, intimacies that even now filled her with heated curiosity.

"As you well know," he continued, using his best 'instructor's' voice. "You may not deny the suit until as such time they address the Queen formally, within your presence. A Request to Court is no more than a form of respect, extended to your Queen, and Lady Mother, from the ruling sect of Wizard Twins. You cannot accept or deny. Only your dear mother," he bowed to Queen Amoria with a surprisingly graceful move, "has this right."

He tilted his head to look at her once again. Brianna frowned darkly at the arrogance in his voice, his stance. The sharp features, leathery and appearing wrinkled as he spoke, gave an impression of superiority, of wisdom. Brianna, in the course of her studies with the dragon, Garron, had often wondered if he hadn't stood before a mirror often to perfect just that certain haughty expression.

"It makes no difference, Dragon," she bit out. "I will not be forced into this alliance, or their perverted desires. What woman would wish this? To be shared? It is not natural."

"Ah, but here many would disagree with you," he instructed, his tone smoothly cultured and grating excessively on her nerves as his thin arms rose, his fingers linking together as he regarded her with an expression of superiority. "It is often debated that the unnatural, for those of the magick sect, is how it stands today. From the creation of the first Wizard Twins they have known but one Sorceress between them. And so it was from the dawn of creation upon this planet, to the time of separation, barely a millennia ago."

"Garron, I did not call you here for a lesson in history," Queen Amoria snapped in a rare display of frustration, her delicate brow creasing in a frown. "I have asked you here to instruct my daughter, privately if you will, on what you know of the Wizard Twins."

Had Brianna not been watching the dragon closely, she would have missed the flare of pain in his bright, black eyes.

"A history lesson." He shrugged negligently as he held Brianna's gaze. "Would you not agree, Princess? I can of course, provide pictures."

Brianna's face flamed.

"A lesson on idiots perhaps," Brianna bit out. "I see no reason for this."

"Because you refuse to." The Queen was becoming impatient now.

Brianna tightened her lips, holding back her furious flood of defense.

"I have decreed, Princess Brianna, that the Wizard Twins be allowed to this year's Covenani Ball. There they may, if they so desire, seek official permission to present suit to you. You will, and this is no request, answer them with a request of your own, to be given a proper amount of time to make such an important decision. It is my decision, as Queen and sole ruler of Covenan, that the time of separation is past. Cauldaran Wizards will no longer be barred from our country, nor our gatherings. You alone, daughter..." she speared Brianna with a sharp, knowing look, "should know the ramifications of this decision."

With no further ado, she stood from her throne and stalked from the room. Brianna was left shocked, surprised, staring at her sister Serena in bewilderment. How was she to know such ramifications? All she knew was that her mother, who until this point had always been loving and protective, was literally throwing her to the monsters. Or did her mother truly believe this was not true?

The elder daughter came to her feet from the elaborate chair that proclaimed her the next in the ruling line. Serena sighed tiredly.

"I would suggest, Brianna," she said softly, "that you consider this matter a bit more than you have at this point. Should you need to talk, you know where I can be found."

She too left the room, leaving Brianna in the company of the dragon. She glanced at him, then sighed herself in frustration. Such an expression of sarcasm. Her mother should reinstate the execution laws while she was at it. Had there ever been a living being who deserved "off with his head" it was this one.

"Do you require manuals?" he asked drolly, producing a stack of books that suddenly appeared at her feet. "Pictures included, my dear. I do remember your joy of them."

Chapter Three

Queen Amoria stood beneath the shelter of the Weeping Tree, more than aware of the dampness on her cheeks and the break in her control. She had left strict orders that no others were to be allowed within the gardens this evening, to assure the privacy she needed as she fought to contain her emotions.

Her daughters were furious with her. Not just Brianna, but Serena and Marina as well. They did not understand her decision, and she did not blame them.

She eased down on the marble bench, sheltered by the cascading branches of the tree. Staring at the crystalline drops of liquid further atop the branches, her heart clenched in agony. The Weeping Tree held tears for her, but would not shed them. Still, the Sorceress Matriarch had not heard her pleas.

Legend said if the Weeping Tree shed its tears for you, then the Sorceress Matriarch would hear your needs and bring to you solace for your sorrow. But Amoria knew there would be no solace for her. Even the Wizard Sentinels and the Sorceress Matriarch would not return the dead.

She lowered her head then, brushing at the betraying drops of liquid that came from her own eyes. She had just, in one proclamation, overturned centuries of peace within the Covenani. She, who had upheld the idea that Sorceresses and Wizard Twins should continue to be separate, had given the strongest of those Twins permission to Join with her daughter.

Had she betrayed Brianna, as she had been accused? Surely not. Garron would not have lied to her about the habits of the Wizards Twins. Indeed, the sexual escapades were more than extreme, but her youngest had a sense of adventure that should serve her well.

Still though, Brianna was terrified, clinging to the rumors of pain and death that the Wizard Twins could bring to their Consorts. She sighed deeply, shaking her head as yet more tears slipped down her cheeks. How she needed D'lyell's advice now. His broad shoulders to cling to. But he was gone. Taken from her when her children were but babes during one of the bloody battles with the Seculars.

And now, the Seculars were taking another loved one from her. Her precious daughter would leave her home now, travel the distance to the Cauldaran lands, and be separated from her.

At one time, when Sentmar and the Sorceresses were stronger, this would have been no problem. But shadowtravel was impossible now. Stepping across the distance of a few acres was incredibly wearing. But shadowtraveling across the mountains was unattainable.

"Self pity is weakening, my Queen." A gasp came from her throat as Garron materialized in front of her.

The huge dragon stared down at her from his lofty height, his black eyes holding an expression of censure and superior knowledge. There had not been a time that the dragon had not grated on her nerves.

"You are treasonously disrespectful," she bit out contemptuously as she came to her feet. "How dare you defy my orders and disturb me here."

He snorted. A completely male sound of irritation that had her fighting a compulsion to tighten her fingers into fists. She refused to display such childish tendencies in his presence.

"I thought you would like an update on your daughter." His voice held equal parts affection and exasperation as he spoke of Brianna. "She is most stubborn, my dear. I can see she is truly your daughter."

Amoria's eyes narrowed. "I rather thought her stubbornness came from her father." She was aware of the softening of her voice, the vein of sadness and regret that whispered through her tone. How she missed D'lyell, and could clearly see his stubbornness in Brianna's violet eyes.

"Hmphf." The dragon snorted again. "Such female tenacity could have come from you only. Despite a clear interest in these Wizards who court her, she has a stranglehold on her fears and refuses to release them. Your plans may go awry do they not arrive soon."

Large leathery wings shifted on the great back as he settled down in front of her, relaxing beneath the cooling shelter of the Weeping Tree. His sharp, scale covered face was turned to her, his large, unblinking eyes regarding her curiously.

Amoria sighed wearily. "They arrive soon," she said bitterly. "A thousand years of peace destroyed. I cannot believe I was the one to set aside all that my ancestors have worked for."

A coughing laugh escaped the dragon. Mocking, sarcastic, the huge beast had little respect for the separation of Covenani and Cauldaran.

"Oh yes, dear Queen," he grumped. "A thousand years of boredom and Secular growth cannot be ignored. Let us regret this day until ever our highest gods reach down and pluck the offenders from our path."

Amoria rolled her eyes at the dragon's droll tone.

"You mock me, Dragon. Such disrespect to your Queen is forbidden."

He tilted his head, watching her with that strange mix of intelligence and amusement.

"So punish me." His great shoulders shrugged negligently. "A public flogging perhaps?" He shivered with a mocking moan. "Whip me, my Queen, whip me."

Amoria nearly laughed at the expression of false pleasure and anticipation that crossed his expression.

"You are a menace," she sighed instead. "You should be banned from Covenan, the same as the Wizards were."

"Ah, but who then would amuse you during your hours of sadness?" he asked her mockingly before turning suddenly serious. "But this is all well and good. I have spent two days with your more than stubborn daughter. I thought perhaps you would like my assessment of this situation now." He watched her inquiringly.

Amoria folded her hands in her lap and watched him with strained patience.

"Proceed." She nodded, ignoring his dragonny grunt of impatience.

"She will accept this situation only when she must," he told her with a rumbled growl that displayed his exasperation with the Princess. "Do not put extra protection around her, and keep that flighty, horror-telling nurse from her rooms at night. That woman delights in grisly tales of blood and murder." He shuddered excessively. "She unsettles even me."

Elspeth was indeed becoming a problem, Amoria knew. She was determined to believe that Wizard Twins had been the ones to rape and murder her child, though Amoria had told her countless times that such a thing was impossible. No magick had touched that young woman, only evil had. An evil that sent a chill down Amoria's back.

"They frightened her, Garron," she reminded him.

"No, my Queen, they pleasured her." He rose to his feet impatiently, his sudden anger confusing her. "She is their Consort, else they could not have done such a thing. I do not agree with, nor condone it, but perhaps it is the only way to settle these visions of blood and death that fill that female mind of hers. Now, you have my assessment. I am weary from dealing with such females and will seek my rest until the Veraga Twins arrive. You may come for me then."

"Come for you?" she bit out, frowning. "I come for no one, Garron…"

"And perhaps this is your problem," he grunted. "Just as Brianna, you have held your lofty power like a miser holds his gold. Be a woman, Amoria. Coming for a man is not such a terrible thing."

Fury flared bright and hot inside her, but before she could flay the scales from his disrespectful hide, he vanished.

"Oh." She stomped her foot in fury as she gazed at the suddenly empty area in front of her. "Damn you, Dragon. Damn your thick male hide."

She consoled herself fleetingly with visions of a stuffed Garron, his eyes wide with horror, gracing the entrance hall to her castle. She gritted her teeth as she fought the flood of anger coursing through her. Damned disrespectful dragon. He was lucky he was the last of his kind. Otherwise, she would be more than tempted to execute his sorry hide, as he more than deserved.

Chapter Four

℘

Brianna watched the Wizards as they arrived in the courtyard, dismounting from the great feathered owls that flew them across the mountains. The Veraga Twins were easily picked out among the large group of more than arrogant Wizard sets. Their broad shoulders and stubborn turn of their heads were distinctive to them.

Their long black hair was tied back at their nape, flowing below their shoulders. They were muscular, well built, handsome and daring, and they terrified her. They made her ache and want, and filled her dreams with such erotic acts that she would awake, her body burning, screaming out for relief. A relief she knew not how to attain.

Even now, the flesh between her thighs pulsed and ached. The hard little button of her clit was swollen, so sensitive she feared the reprisals should she touch it. It would surely burst in an agony of pain as Elspeth had always predicted would happen should their magick touch her. And she feared it touched her often. Nightly, at least.

Her hand clenched on the sill of the window as she continued to watch them, listening to their deep, raised voices as they called out orders and prepared to release the great owls until they needed them once again.

The huge beasts nested in the Laughing Mountains to the North of Covenan, and made themselves available to the Wizards of Cauldaran exclusively. Only the female owls had ever carried the Wizards. Their strong, sturdy bodies bearing the burden of the warriors and ruling Wizards with strength and grace. It was said they were fierce and savage in battle as well. They were protective of their burdens, and were said to be more than willing to give their lives to save those who rode upon their backs.

Garron had assured her that before the separation of the magick sects, the owls had not been needed to carry the Wizards into battle. Indeed, there had been few battles because the magick of Covenani and Cauldaran had kept the lands balanced and in harmony. Brianna scoffed at this, though. If this were true, why then had the Sorceresses separated from the bold, arrogant Wizards? This was a question no one could, or would answer.

"So they have arrived." Elspeth's furtive, hate filled voice hissed from behind her. "May the Sorceress Matriarch bless you, my Princess. How could your mother have betrayed you in this fashion?"

Brianna bit her lip nervously.

"Garron assures her I will be treated well by them," Brianna told her as they watched the commotion below. "I am not being forced..."

"You are, Princess," Elspeth protested fearfully. "Neither you nor your mother knows the trickery of these fiends. You must run from them. Hide. You cannot let them destroy you."

Brianna stilled the welling fear that rose inside her. Garron, though mocking and sarcastic, had never lied to her, nor led her astray. He had sworn on his dragon's heart, that the Wizards would not, could not harm her.

"Let us see what happens," Brianna said quietly. "You had best return to your home, Elspeth. You know Mother said you are not to be here for now. I think this is too painful for you."

She glanced at Elspeth sympathetically as the older woman gazed with hatred and malice at the men below.

"I must save you," Elspeth whispered. Despite the tone of fear and worry in the nurse's voice, Brianna felt a flare of unease.

"I will be fine, Elspeth," she promised her as the owls lifted off from the courtyard and filled the skies as they searched for a place of rest until the Wizards needed them once again. "I must go to the Receiving Hall now. Return to your home as Mother bid you. I will check on you soon."

Brianna turned from the window and moved quickly for the stairs that led to the great Receiving Hall. She had fought bitterly to miss the reception, but her mother had been adamant that she be there.

Serena and Marina were there ahead of her. Her two older sisters were dressed, the same as Brianna, in their ceremonial gowns of white and sapphire blue. The delicate fabric skimmed their bodies, falling to their feet in graceful folds of the purest white. Soft, sapphire blue edging, and embroidered starbursts along the shoulders and hemline proclaimed their status. On their heads they wore their small crowns of gold and glittering *dialmas* stones, though Serena, as next in line to rule, wore a crown slightly larger than her sisters.

As Brianna stepped in line beside her sister, she lowered her head beneath her mother's gentle regard.

"Queen Amoria, the Wizards of Cauldaran extend their thanks for your invitation and request entrance into your home, and your grace." A Sentinel guard stepped forth with the traditional greeting.

"You have my permission to enter. My home is yours, for as long as your stay should last," Queen Amoria answered regally.

Brianna felt her stomach drop. There were more than a dozen Wizard sets, as well as the Sentinel Guards, the warriors of Cauldaran. There were forty males altogether.

Tall, handsome, powerful. The air was suddenly thick with an energy Brianna couldn't define as they began to enter the Castle, their messenger introducing each on entrance.

Sandalwood and spice, and an elixir of excitement wrapped about the proceedings. As though the added power of the male magick had suddenly transformed her home and made it a mysterious, exciting place to be. She wasn't certain she liked the feeling.

Finally, the Veraga Wizards, rulers and holders of the Cauldaran Scepter, stepped forth and were announced. Brianna barely contained her whimper as something flared deep within her woman's core. A heat she couldn't ignore that flushed her body and filled her blood with power. She could feel energy crackling around her, sensitizing her flesh.

"Princess Brianna." They stepped before her, staring down at her, one with eyes of the deepest blue and filled with lust and carnal needs. The other's eyes of green, filled with compassion, warmth, and needs she didn't want to define.

"I welcome you to the Palace of the Covenani," she whispered, mortified at the trembling of her voice as she lowered herself into a graceful curtsey before them.

"You lower yourself before us no more." Drago's blue eyes flared as her surprised gaze rose to his. He had not made such a demand of her sisters before her.

He gripped her arm as she rose, trembling before him. Before her stunned gaze, both Wizards went to their knees, bowing gracefully, humbly.

"We are at your service, Sorceress," Lasan said deeply as Brianna's confused gaze swung to her mother.

She felt as though she were suffocating on the power surrounding her. Her heart was thundering, the blood rushing through her veins in demand. But a demand for what, she was not certain. Confusion filled the women, but it tore through Brianna like the great winds of the Wintry Mountains.

They were waiting. Kneeling at her feet, heads lowered as she trembled before them. Fear rushed through her as something seemed to build within her. A surge of power she had never known, feared she did not want. She shook her head, the faces of Wizards and Sorceresses watching her expectantly, moving dizzyingly around her.

She heard a whimper, barely realizing it was her own as she felt her sisters move beside her. A static sound of energy sounded in her ears, thundered through her body. To her utter horror and humiliation she felt her cunt seep with a rush of fluids as the power thundering through her body began to center in her woman's core. Her eyes widened, she trembled, her hands clenching as she fought...

The pulse of pleasure that flooded her body had a small cry tearing past her lips as her clit exploded and her cunt rained with the soft juices of a release that thundered her body. She staggered, nearly losing her balance as she distantly heard her mother's demand for answers.

Lasan and Drago looked up at her, sensuality and carnal pleasure filled their expressions.

"No." She stumbled back, fighting against the weakness that suddenly filled her, the overriding need to step forward, to plead for mercy.

Confused, distraught with her lack of control, she felt tears fill her eyes as she struggled for control, for strength to get away from them.

"Princess, be at ease," Lasan whispered gently, compassion filling his voice. "Allow your power..."

"No!" Brianna cried out as his voice seemed to intensify the coursing pleasure that thundered through her blood.

Her eyes went to her mother, as fear flamed as high as desire.

Queen Amoria watched with anger and confusion. As though in slow motion Brianna watched her mother step to her, then stop, fury flashing across her face as though some unseen force had halted her movements.

She could feel her juices trickling along her female nether lips and need spiraling once again in her body. She would be screaming out for ease again in seconds. The fear of that seared her brain. Calling on every incantation she had ever been taught she fought to break the magick that wrapped around her with velvet bands of pleasure.

"Do not touch her." Drago turned suddenly from her, his eyes glowing with a mixture of sexual pleasure and fury as Marina and Serena moved to her side.

As his attention splintered, Brianna broke from the hold. Shaking, her body on fire with mingled terror and lust, she gazed at them in horrified confusion.

"You are demons," she cried out frantically, stumbling back, barely catching herself on the dragon that had suddenly materialized behind her. "Garron." She gripped his sturdy leg, using his broad body to find a sense of balance. "Please," she whispered, knowing his power, beseeching him now as fear filled her. "Please, Garron, help me."

Before she could blink, it was over. She had never shadowtraveled in her life, but within seconds the curious, intent faces of those in the Receiving Hall had disappeared, and she was standing unsteadily in her room, gripping the dragon's leg as she fought for her control.

Menage A Magick

"I warned you," Garron said in exasperation. "You do not heed my words, and you do not listen to my advice. This, Princess, is what happens when you ignore me."

She vaguely remembered a lecture on her first meeting with the Wizards.

"Sorceresses," Garron bit out with such a tone of male frustration that she winced.

He paced away from her, his talons making a soft, comforting scrape against the stone floor.

"What did they do to me?" She twisted her hands together nervously.

"They did nothing," he growled. "Your power did this, and had you just listened to me…" His voice rose with his male anger. "No one listens to me. I am a dragon. Ageless. Knowing secrets you cannot imagine." If he had hair, Brianna was certain he would be pulling it out. "Yet you and that stubborn mother of yours never listen. You never heed my advice. Never pay attention." He snarled in anger.

"My power has never done such things," she argued furiously. "Why would it do so now?"

"Because, woman—" he growled, but was interrupted when the door flew open.

"Dragon, you are needed." Drago, Lasan, and Queen Amoria stood in the doorway. "The Princess's mother can comfort her. We require you at this moment."

Garron's eyes narrowed and his scales seemed to hiss with impatience.

"You require me?" he asked silkily.

Brianna blinked at the insolence in his tone. There was a challenge in his voice that none could mistake.

Drago frowned. "Aye, Dragon, I require your presence now."

35

The Twins turned and left the room, arrogance seething around them. Brianna's gaze went to the dragon. He glanced at her, his eyes still narrowed.

"I now remember why I sleep for such long periods," he grunted. " Wizard Twins are more unsettling than Matriarch Sorceresses. Damned prideful males."

In a blink he disappeared. Brianna turned to her mother, crossed her arms over her chest and announced with all the determination she could muster, "I refuse to Consort with demons. I deny their suit." Such intensity of emotion and heights of reaction within a woman's body could not be good. Could it?

Amoria sighed.

Chapter Five

ॐ

The yearly Covenani Ball was in full swing. The royal palace was filled, all three ballrooms were in use, and the belle of the year was none other than Brianna Sellane, third daughter to the throne of the Covenan. Not that Brianna had any designs on said throne. She would have preferred to give up her chair at the Coven Council, but some things one did not do. Giving away her heritage being the first, her mother had informed her.

The annual ball for unmarried Covenani females was another. This was Brianna's third year, an almost unheard of total. It was also the first year in over a millennia that the Wizards of Cauldaran were in attendance. Brianna cursed that particular decision. Twin Wizards now roamed the halls and the ballrooms. Brooding in looks, sexy and powerful, they completely overshadowed their human male counterparts. They would have stolen the attention of the unattached females were it not for the fact that Covenani females had no desire to lose their power and their independence in the face of such males.

This night, the Veraga Twins were at the ball as well. Their eyes followed her, watched her. Brianna was uncomfortably aware of the arousal in her body from that knowledge. Her cunt pulsed, her clit ached, remembered pulses of tormenting pleasure pounded through her blood. What had they done to her upon their arrival?

She had avoided them in the past three days, since that humiliating meeting at the Receiving Hall. Had stayed far away, and fought the needs that churned inside her. Vague dreams flitted through her mind, visions of sexual excesses that both terrified and aroused her.

Her nurse had described such sex acts as painful. Horrendous. Capable of tearing a woman in two when their cocks invaded her simultaneously. And though the thought of that possession filled her with fear, it also filled her with lust.

"The Veraga Twins are still watching you, Bri," her sister Serena said with amused concern.

"I am aware of that," Brianna sighed. She could feel their gazes on her, stroking her with heated looks.

She fought to ignore what this did to her body. Fought to ignore the ache of need that had not completely abated since they had knelt at her feet days before.

She glanced at her older, beautiful sister and wished she possessed a tenth of Serena's bearing and poise. She could have easily handled the Wizard Twins and sent them scurrying out of sight. That is, if anyone could. It would have been hard for even the most self-possessed woman to send the leaders of the vast Wizard sect running. The Veraga Wizards were immovable objects when they decided on something. And they had decided on Brianna months before.

"Mother is very much for this alliance, Bri," Serena told her quietly. "I cannot understand why, but she thinks it would be in the best interests of the Covenani to consider it."

Brianna flinched. She was very well aware of her mother's opinion of this. Just as her mother should be well aware of hers by now. Even Garron had finally given up, and merely frowned at her in disapproval now. A dragon's frown was not the most comfortable sight.

She glanced at the Veraga Twins once again. They were so broad, so handsome and muscular it made her teeth clench in fury. The human females flitted around them like birds to nectar, and set her nerves on edge. Demons that those two were, they were likely teasing the silly twits with whatever power they had used on her.

"I will not submit to those two," Brianna hissed furiously. "I have heard the tales of their unnatural desires, as have you. Why would mother wish to send me to such a hellish existence?"

The question had plagued her for days now, ever since her mother's first words giving her blessing to the alliance should Brianna consider it. Queen Amoria had only scoffed at the tales Brianna recounted to her, but finally admitted she knew only that the Veraga Wizards had sworn on their oath that Brianna would come to no harm. They did not deny, though, that she would sleep in a bed that both males would share with her. Together.

And yet, neither could Brianna control the flare of lust that sang through her body each time they were near. Either separately or apart, it made no difference. Her body hungered for them.

"They have assured Mother of your future happiness and security, Brianna, you can ask no more of them than that," her sister told her.

"I do not wish to hear this." Brianna shook her head in denial. "I have told Mother and now I will tell you. I will not be a Consort to ones such as the Veraga Twins. I do not know why the two of you will not drop this."

A delicate frown creased Serena's pale brow. Her lavender colored eyes darkened a bit with her worry. Serena was the most beautiful of the ruling house of Sellane. With her long auburn curls, milk-white skin and unusual eyes, she drew both male and female looks of approval. She was a wonderful sister as well, until she found a subject worthy of her stubbornness. As she had now.

"Brianna, perhaps it would be worth considering," Serena said worriedly. "Mother is certain the rumors of any pain are unfounded, and we are being threatened by the humans outside our own province. The Seculars in particular are arming for battle. We could use the strength—"

"The Seculars have armed before." Brianna shrugged, though this news worried her as well. "Say no more of this, Serena. My heart is not in this alliance you and Mother would wish. I will not give in to your pleas."

Chapter Six

๛

Brianna turned away from her sister and headed for the silence and hopefully the privacy of the gardens. She had lied to her sister, and she knew this well. Her heart beat faster when in the presence of the Wizards, her body heated and longed for them in the darkness of night, but she could not imagine giving herself heart and soul, as Cauldaran males demanded.

She slipped into the velvety shadows of the night, the gardens welcoming her, the scents of blooming night flowers and the sultry heat of the darkness embracing her with tendrils of sensuality.

The thin fabric of her gown seemed confining as it stretched across her breasts and brushed over her abdomen and thighs. Her flesh demanded that she release the ties at her shoulders and allow the silken fabric to fall to her feet, but she refrained from such a move. Roaming naked through the gardens was all well and good, but only when there were no Veraga Wizards around to take advantage of such a move. Not, she figured, that clothes would do her much good against their determination.

* * * * *

Drago and Lasan watched Brianna leave the ballroom, following her every move until she was out of sight with a sense of hunger that burned in their loins. The pure white of her gown skimmed from her full breasts to her dainty toes, outlining the curvaceous, tempting body it covered. Her power was nearing its full strength. Soon, she would

41

come into a phase where it would be all or nothing. Were they not there to share in the surge of white-hot energy and magick absorption, then they would never forge the bond with her that was imperative between Cauldaran and Covenani Consorts. Wizards and Sorceress must come together at the exact time, during the peak of her energy level. That time was nearing. It showed in the glitter of her violet eyes, the restlessness of her walk and the peak hardness of her nipples whenever they neared her.

But most surprising of all had been the flare of corresponding power that had surged from her to both Drago and Lasan when they had knelt before her. Observing the old rules of Binding, Drago and Lasan had knelt before the one the Wizard Sentinels had assured them was their true Consort. Shock, and a pleasure unlike anything they had known had immediately surged through them.

By placing themselves beneath her, and centering their power on her, it had allowed the matching female center of her magick to flare outward, connecting and centering within their own male force. The reaction had nearly been climactic. Lasan well understood why such practices were observed in only the strictest settings before the separation of the Covenani and Cauldaran.

It had, unfortunately, embarrassed and frightened their Consort, though. Which was making the courtship proceed at a ridiculously slow pace. She had refused to so much as be in the same room with them since that day.

She was their natural Consort. Created for them alone by the gods. They had feared it would be impossible to gauge the time of her magick fertility so well. But even so, she was wary and frightened, knowing little of their ways, and it was forbidden that they should explain it to her.

The magick of their planet, Sentmar, was steeped in mystery to most. Only a certain handful of the Wizard Twins were given the knowledge to gauge the wondrous gifts that the planet could bestow upon them. It was the energy of the gods. It flowed from the very ground they stood upon, lingered in the air, filled every cavern and flowed through every drop of water. But only a few were deemed deserving to know the secret of drawing it forth. Lasan and Drago were two of those that the all-powerful Wizard Sentinels had come to, to tutor in the ways of Sentmar magick.

One of those lessons had been the bond that tied Wizard Twins and Covenani Sorceress. Each was separate parts of the same magick. The Wizard Sentinels directed male magick, the Sorceress Matriarchs directed the female sect. If the two remained separated, then the magick that filled their planet would slowly weaken. For one was ineffective without the other. A thousand years of separation had allowed the humans in the far provinces to gain ground already. They could allow this to go on no longer.

To reunite the two, the Wizard Sentinels had informed Lasan and Drago of the one Sorceress created to be their other half. A gift from the Sorceress Matriarch to the Wizard sect. That woman was Brianna, the most wary and stubborn of the ruling house of Sellane.

"She's frightened," Lasan murmured to his twin as he watched Brianna stalk from the crowded room.

"But receptive." There was a trace of satisfaction in Drago's voice. He burned for her, just as Lasan did. The fire threatened, on more than one occasion, to consume them and to rush the completion of their mating with her.

The fear she displayed concerned them. They marked it down, though, to fear of the unknown.

"Receptive is not always enough," Lasan warned him with an edge of worry. Drago's inclination to rush her could be their downfall if they were not extremely careful.

He could feel his brother's impatience beating at him, feeding his own. It was their curse; Wizard twins were receptive to each other in ways that most others could never understand. They were two halves of a whole, in strengths as well as weaknesses. They knew each other's hungers, dreams and desires, shared them and fought for them. And they knew the same sexual needs. Those needs had focused on Brianna Sellane.

"She hungers for us as well, Lasan," Drago murmured in lustful satisfaction as he glanced over at him. "I can feel her heat whenever we are near her."

And she did burn. They were more than aware of the heat and hunger she was not yet experienced enough to hide.

"Will you go to her, or should I?" Drago asked, though they both knew the answer. They could ill afford to push her into a reckless course of action right now.

Taking a deep, control-fortifying breath, Lasan followed her. They knew that for this night, Drago's forceful personality would only frighten her further. His body was hard, his cock pounding, the blood thrumming through his veins at the thought of catching her alone in the gardens. A chance to touch her silken skin, to inhale the sweet scent that was hers alone. Perhaps to taste her, hear her throaty moans of pleasure. He had been unable to do that but once in the past year that they had sought to court her. Not that Lasan was better off, but his natural patience made him the less volatile of the two.

Brianna Sellane was a most difficult female to court. She had outright refused them after their first overture during a Covenani visit to the Wizards' lands. Her decision had not changed, despite repeated journeys by them to the Covenani Palace and the Queen's acceptance of their attentions to her daughter. The woman ran from them at every chance. She sneered at their desire for her and ridiculed their proposal. The time would come and soon, were she not careful, when she would not be in a position of such easy denial.

Lasan found her alone as he had hoped. Wrapped in the night, her flame red hair falling down her back, caressing her hips. Her back was to him as she stared up at the twin moons of their world. Lasan could feel the sadness of her thoughts, but not the reason for them. That sadness pricked at him and he knew Drago felt it as well. They would have her filled with happiness and laughter, not gazing into the stars as she sought answers to questions that disturbed her.

"They say it is the twin moons that decide the births of the Wizards," Lasan reflected as he moved up behind her. "Displease the gods of the moons and no twins will be born of your Consort's womb."

He watched her stiffen, felt the air shimmer with her nervousness. She turned slowly, staring up at him, then beside him, then peeking around him. In confusion, Lasan glanced back, but saw nothing to explain her actions.

"Where's your shadow?" she finally asked him, her voice filled with ire.

Lasan's lips quirked in amusement as he felt Drago's snort of disgust at her words. "Drago is still entertaining the various human women your mother and sister have thrown at us since our arrival. Would you like me to call him to us? I am certain he would be more than pleased—"

"No." She shook her head quickly. "Why don't you join him? I'm sure there's enough women surrounding him for the both of you."

She spoke with insulting ease of them going to others for their satisfaction, yet Lasan saw the flare of anger in the crystalline depths of her violet eyes.

She may speak easily of it, but he knew she had no desire to see either of them falling for the attention of any of the human females who watched them with lustful, greedy gazes.

"We would prefer to surround you, dearest Brianna," he told her, allowing his voice to soften with the gentleness he felt for her. "Yet you run from us at every chance."

She frowned up at him. Her fingers gripped a small fold of her dress, creasing it with her nervous movements.

"I do not wish to be a Consort to you and your brother," she bit out. "What must I do to convince you of this, Lasan?"

Lasan sighed deeply. He could hear the fear in her voice and that hurt him as nothing else could. They did not want her to know fear, only happiness. The centuries the Covenani had spent away from their natural partners had instilled a growing wariness in their females that was damned near impossible to breech.

"To convince us, do not tremble when we are near, Brianna," he told her, his voice soft as he moved closer to her. His hand reached out, cupping her neck, as he demanded she hold his gaze. "To convince us, do not let your nipples harden until they are nearly cutting through the cloth of your dress and do not let your eyes darken, betraying your thoughts, your curiosity."

Her breath caught. Lasan glanced down, seeing the hard tips of her nipples beneath the cloth. He wanted to groan in hunger. He wanted to pull the cloth away from those generous mounds and taste every sweet inch of skin.

"You are bewitching me." He could hear the confusion in her voice, her fear of her own responses.

"I do not bewitch you, dearest," he assured her. "You know a Wizard cannot ensnare the Covenani through magick or any other means. Especially not one their hearts, bodies and minds have chosen as a Consort. Your own Sorceress Matriarch forbids it."

Beneath his palm, the blood thundered through her veins. She was aroused and fighting it with all the determination her youth could afford her. Lasan was certain it would not be enough to sustain her in this battle of desire.

"I do not wish to be your Consort," she bit out roughly, jerking away from him.

Lasan sighed with weariness. His body ached with need for her. His soul clenched with the power he would give her on their Joining. She did not know what she refused from him. And he could not tell her.

"Brianna." Lasan fought to keep his impatience under control. His needs, Drago's needs, they beat at his brain, making control a bitter beast to master. "Choosing a Consort is not a matter of just what we would wish. Do you know how difficult, how rare it is, for Wizard Twins to find their one true Consort? The woman who meets both their desires and needs?"

He moved to her once again, his hands settling on her bare shoulders, his palms soaking in the warmth of her, the heat of desire and of fear. The intensity of her own needs frightened her as much as any he and Drago had.

"Do I act as though I care?" she snapped. "I am not your Consort, so it makes no difference to me."

Her denial pricked a vein of impatience that Lasan did not know he possessed.

"We want to touch you, Bri," he told her, needing to make her understand. "We need to hold you, love you. You are a part of us, and you don't even realize it."

47

Her violet eyes flashed in the moonlight when she turned back to him. Power surged through her body, causing Lasan's cock to tighten with a desperate need to share that surge of energy with her.

"And do my needs, my wants not matter?" she questioned him fiercely. "Am I permitted to decide for myself who I shall Consort with?"

Lasan stepped forward closely, watching as she backed up. She moved hesitantly, almost fearfully, until with a gasp, the thick trunk of the tree behind her stopped her retreat.

"Does your cunt not throb with need for us?" he asked her as he stopped, barely a breath from her body.

Lasan looked down, watching as her breasts rose and fell rapidly, her hard nipples so close to brushing his chest that all he had to do was breathe deeply to meet the contact.

"It is not natural," she whispered, shaking her head, trembling before him.

Triumph exploded in his loins. He knew Drago was slowly making his way from the ballroom, unable to stop his need to join them, to touch her, to be a part of this initial bonding. It was too natural to them. Too much a part of who they were.

"It is entirely natural, Brianna," he soothed her softly, his hands going to her arms as he pulled her against him. "Drago and I are a gift to you from the Wizard Sentinels, just as you are a gift to us from your Matriarch Sorceress. There is nothing so natural as this need that courses through your body."

He felt her breathing accelerate further, felt the heat of her body, the fierce throb of her desire echoing beneath his flesh. She stared up at him, her violet eyes glittering in the darkness, her flesh kissed by moonlight, shimmering with satin translucence.

As he moved her carefully, positioning her to allow Drago to ease into their embrace, his hand came up, cupping her soft cheek. She bewitched him. She accomplished what he and Drago were only accused of. She mesmerized them, staring up, so innocent, half fearful, half curious, all woman.

"I hunger for you," he whispered. "Since the moment my eyes touched yours, I have hungered, Brianna, in ways you could never know."

He watched her swallow tightly, her tongue moving to dampen her lips. That small action had his cock jerking in need. He wanted her to lick his lips, his body. Sweet Matriarch, she was destroying him.

Chapter Seven

∞

Brianna wanted to fight. She was desperate to still the frightening, surging sensations inside her own body. Even more terrifying than the tales Elspeth had told her was this shattering lack of self-control. She could not make herself step back from him. Could not command her voice to deny him. She stared into those brilliant green eyes, drowning in the sensual, erotic heat that surrounded her.

"You terrify me," she whispered weakly as his thumb whispered over her lips. She couldn't deny herself a taste of him. Her tongue stroked the pad of his thumb, some wicked part of her glorying in his harsh male groan.

"I want only to please you," he said, his voice low, dark with sensual promise. "We, Brianna. We want only to please you."

She felt Drago at her back, her eyes widening as warm male lips stroked over her shoulder. She trembled, her body flushing, heating as she shook within their grip.

"Lasan." She gripped his arms tightly, fighting to stand steady as fear rippled through her senses.

"Easy, Brianna." He steadied her, holding her close as Drago repeated his whispered caress along her other shoulder. "We will not harm you, precious. Never would we harm you. Just allow us next to you, Brianna. That is all. Just a few stolen moments of your time."

Her nails bit into his arms as she fought herself as well as them. She could not succumb, she cried out silently. They would destroy her. Steal her will and then her life.

"Oh, Matriarch," she cried out breathlessly as she felt Drago's tongue paint a path of fire behind her ear.

Her entire body trembled. Heat exploded in her womb, and she felt that rush of moisture between her thighs, a building intensity of need that she could not deny.

"'Tis natural," Lasan groaned, his lips at her brow, warm and heated. "This time is for you, Brianna. To assure you there is no pain in our arms. No reason to fear. Until the night of our Joining…"

They push their cocks inside you, Princess, simultaneously. Taking you from front and behind, tearing you in two, ripping you asunder as they did my baby… Elspeth's words suddenly tore through her mind.

Gasping, fear now rising as hard and fierce as her desire to submit, Brianna tore away from them, stumbling several feet from where they watched her, confusion etched on their features.

"Brianna?" Lasan whispered her name carefully.

"One," she bit out. "Promise me. Just one of you, and I will submit to the Joining."

She could no longer deny that she ached for their touch, that she needed whatever sensation was rising so hot and strong inside her, but she would not endure the pain she knew it would bring.

"Brianna, you know this is impossible," Drago sighed roughly. "There can be no Joining except that which our natures decree."

"Your nature, not mine." She shook her head, denying the velvet plea in his voice. "I have no desire to be torn asunder by the two of you. Decide now. One or none. Your choice."

She was shaking, trembling so hard her teeth were nearly chattering. Lasan appeared confused, but Drago, damn his hide, he smiled mockingly, knowingly.

"We accept neither term," he said softly, promisingly. "No, Brianna. Both of us. Together."

"I refuse." She wanted to smack the confidence from his face. "You do not dictate to me, Drago. I will not have it."

"Dictate to you?" he flared in frustration. "It would seem to me that it is you attempting to dictate nature. You cannot do this, Brianna. This is not your choice, nor is it ours. We will Join. Together."

The utter arrogance in his voice was too much to bear.

"We shall see about that." She flipped her hair over her shoulder, facing them furiously. "Short of rape, you have no choice. I deny you, Lasan and Drago, and your suit. There will be no Joining."

Before they could deny her, before they could reach out to her and drag her back into the maze of pleasure and sensation that threatened to destroy her, Brianna ran. She turned, moving quickly through the gardens, nearly running in her attempt to escape, not just the Wizards, but her own needs as well.

* * * * *

"Well, you pulled that one off wonderfully." Garron materialized in the space Brianna had previously held, staring at the Wizard Twins in lofty superiority. "Did I not tell you she would not heel as easily as you predicted?"

Drago narrowed his eyes on the beast. He would have sent a burst of magick that would bring the great dragon to its knees, but he knew already such a move was ineffectual.

Drago had tried it once already, only to suffer its mocking amusement.

"Dragon, you are a menace," Lasan sighed. "What happened to her? One moment her power was perfectly aligned with ours, then next, it was as though it had never been."

"That one is not one of your weak-kneed, eager human females," the dragon snorted, earning him a dark glare from Drago. "It amazes me that your race has survived the centuries," Garron continued with an edge of disbelief in his voice. "You cannot rush her…"

"Her power is peaking," Drago bit out forcefully. "We cannot wait much longer. If she passes her peak without the Joining, then all is lost."

The bond was too important, imperative actually, in the future happiness of Wizard Twins and Sorceress units. This was the mistake their ancestors had made, in Joining before or after the peak of female power. Anticipation, and a lack of control had earned them nothing but the separation that now risked the entire planet.

"Frighten her, and she will run," Garron warned them. "Already her fears have her near hysteria. She is the first in a thousand years to Consort with Wizard Twins, at least have the patience to gauge your steps accordingly."

His lecturing tone indicated a belief that he felt he was talking to children. Lasan arched his brow as he glanced at Drago, catching the narrow-eyed look of irritation on his brother's face.

"I thought dragons were supposed to be extinct," Drago said with tight-lipped control.

Lasan shrugged. "At least now we know why they likely died out. I say they were murdered in desperation. Such an irritating presence would inspire Sentinel Wizards to killing."

Garron sneered. Just as quickly as he had arrived, he was once again gone.

Lasan sighed.

"Perhaps tomorrow she will be more amiable to our presence," he told his brother wearily.

Drago snorted, a sound much too similar to the dragon's.

"We can hope, anyway," he growled.

"Aye," Lasan agreed, though he felt there was little sense in wasting the effort. "We can definitely hope."

Chapter Eight

ᔢ

The next morning, Brianna moved carefully through the halls of the castle, on a careful lookout for Wizard Twins. Not that the place wasn't teeming with them, she thought irritably. Her home had turned into a sanctuary for big, horny magick males who had nothing better to do than accost the innocent Sorceresses who lived within its halls.

It was disgusting, watching them enchant and bewitch her cousins and friends. The silly twits appeared to have not a thought in their heads. Laughing and giggling and appearing comfortable and relaxed in the shelter of two male bodies that dwarfed them, sheltered them.

She turned the corner quickly to the servants' stairs as she heard a heavy, determined tread rounding the hall above her. The stairs were narrow, steeper than those more commonly used. It didn't matter, she told herself as she made her way carefully down them. All that mattered was avoiding a certain Wizard set and finding just a moment of peace to calm her nerves.

No matter where she turned now, it seemed those damned Veraga Twins were awaiting her. She had spent long, tense hours avoiding their touch and their demands. Not that they said much, their eyes, and their expressions said it all. They were determined to claim her. She was just as determined to thwart them.

The kitchen area was busy, bustling with cooks and maids preparing the coming dinner. Little attention was paid to her as she moved quickly through the large room, then exited out the door that led outside.

The sun was a warm, golden orb within the sky, shining down with a heated caress that reminded her much too well of the Wizards' touch. Damned men, she cursed them again.

She smoothed the folds of her emerald green gown over her stomach, only then realizing how similar in color it was to Lasan's eyes. She had rejected several of her favorite dresses that morning for the simple fact that they were the color of Drago's eyes. She would burn every blue and green gown she possessed, she swore.

The soft, clinging material was held in place by a single shoulder band, leaving her other shoulder bare. It cupped her firm breasts and fell in a graceful flow to her feet. A golden cord bound the fabric from her waist to just below her breasts, giving her waist a delicate appearance. Unfortunately, the sleek softness of the material caressed her skin. Skin too sensitized, too tender for such a caress to be comfortable.

Her nipples were beaded, hard little points that ached for attention. Her breasts were swollen, and the flesh between her thighs ached. She was slick and wet there, the lips of her cunt swollen, heated. Her clit was an ache that was ready to drive her to distraction. If she did not find relief soon, she would expire from the need.

As she sought a sheltered, cool area within the gardens to relax, she moved deeper and deeper through the thick, vibrant bushes and low trees that created a haven of relaxing scents and gentle arbors created to soothe the soul. As she moved deeper into the shadows a sudden sense of being watched began to fill her.

Brianna paused, frowning. Drago and Lasan would have shown themselves by now. They would not hide and try to frighten her. They were too bold for such maneuvers.

As she turned to head back to the safety of the more open area, she stopped in sudden fear.

Before her, three human males stood. Their expressions were dark, forbidding. Brianna swallowed tightly. She was not yet in control of the full use of her power, and would have little defenses against them.

"You are forbidden within these gardens," she informed them, fighting to hide her nervousness.

The apparent leader, the largest of the three, sneered at her declaration.

"Seculars are forbidden in many places, Princess. It has not stopped us before."

Terror whipped through Brianna. The cruel sneers, dark, malicious eyes and big tense bodies assured her that they meant to carry out the threat. The dagger the leader held in his clenched fist only underscored the threat.

"How did you get in here?" She stepped back, knowing she could never outrun them.

Fury raged inside her. The Seculars had killed her father when she was but a child. They were animals who hid in waiting, killing in secrecy, never facing the warriors who fought for peace within the land. Brianna knew now that her hopes that they had been defeated in those battles after her father's death were unfounded. She should have heeded her mother's warnings that they were growing in power, in numbers. But had she done so, then she would have to agree to the Joining without a fight.

She trembled, fear and self-recriminations rising inside her.

"We have our ways of getting what we want," the leader assured her as the other two broke off slowly, moving in position to stand beside her. She was breathing hard now, fighting for air as the rage surged inside her.

Like white-hot heat, it began to sear her brain, pulsing through her body as she called upon the few incantations of protectiveness that she knew.

Her powers were so weak. Until she reached maturity, until the peak of her energy flared inside her, then she was little more than helpless in the face of danger.

Where were Drago and Lasan when she needed them? She cursed bitterly. Damned Wizards. They harassed her when she begged for peace, and now that they were needed they were no place to be found.   .

"You can't escape." The brute laughed at her, shaking his head as she continued to back away from them.

The dagger raised, the two coming in at her side narrowed their eyes, their bodies tensing to attack.

"You will die for this," she assured them bitterly. "You will not escape."

Laughter, low and wicked was their reply before they charged.

"Drago!" She screamed out the name of the only warrior she knew fierce enough, savage enough to defend her. Where in the two moons was he now that she needed him?

* * * * *

Drago! Her voice screamed through Drago and Lasan's minds. Terror-filled, her energy and power blood red with her rage and her desperation. They didn't stop to speak, to warn or to order. Simultaneously they sent out the call to the Sentinel guards as they sprinted from the main hall of the castle, ignoring the startled questions of the Queen and the Princess Serena.

They tore through the castle, following the remnants of pain, the magickal bond she had created in a burst of fear.

Terror pounded through their bodies. What if they were not in time? They could feel her life force, holding steady, desperate, then in a flash, brutal and cold, her desperate cries were silent.

Drago was aware of his cry as he sprinted into the back gardens. The echo of a fierce, savage dragon cry vibrated through the enclosed perimeter, fueling his need for added speed.

Garron was enraged. They heard screams, but not cries of a woman's fears. It was the male cries of pain that lingered beneath the earth shattering savagery of the dragon's war cries.

"Secure the area," Drago screamed out to the Sentinel guards as they converged around him. "No one in, no one out."

He and Lasan tore through the underbrush, fighting their way through the quickest route to where they knew Brianna would be. Hot energy flowed through their bodies, the air crackling with emerald green and sapphire blue bolts of energy as a final cry faded into silence.

As Drago tore around the last bend, he ignored the enraged dragon, his eyes going instead to the fragile, fallen form of his Consort.

"Brianna," he screamed her name as he slid to his knees beside her, only distantly aware of the sharp, blood soaked talons of the dragon's foot beside him.

She was gripping the dragon's leg, blood marring her forehead and the side of her face, a ragged slash cut into her chest. Sweet merciful Sentinels, they had tried to cut her heart from her chest.

She breathed. Her chest moved, a whimpering moan sounded from her lips. Drago tore his shirt from his body in a single movement, binding the wound, his hands shaking, fear thundering through his body as the green and blue auras of his and Lasan's magick wrapped around her.

"The liquid silver pools," Garron's voice was imperative, savagely commanding as Drago lifted her into his arms, coming to his feet in a single bound.

"Where are they?" Drago bit out, staring up at the blood stained mouth and sharp teeth of an enraged dragon.

"Hold to me, we shadowwalk."

There was no time to debate the matter. The liquid silver pools were the magick of the gods and there was nothing or no one that could heal her faster. Within seconds, they were deep beneath the bowels of the castle, in a large grotto of multi-colored gems and precious stones.

Drago and Lasan barely noticed the shimmer of silver light that reflected along the walls and ceiling as they quickly removed Brianna's gown. Next came their own clothing, fast, furious, taking no time to care if seams ripped or buttons tore. Time was of the essence now. The ragged wound was steadily seeping her life force, making her weaker by the second.

Within seconds, Drago was easing himself carefully into the pool, steeling himself against the incredible pleasure that began to surround him the further he immersed himself in it.

Lasan eased Brianna into his arms, then quickly followed. Neither Wizard was prepared for the incredible surge of power and pleasure that wrapped around them.

Brianna moaned as they eased her into the gently swirling liquid. Her head fell back on Drago's shoulder, her arms lying lax at her side as they immersed her to her neck, praying they had reached her in time.

Chapter Nine

ഉ

"Drago? Is she well?" Queen Amoria and the two Princesses had entered the grotto without their knowledge. So intent had they been on Brianna, that they had never known of the dragon's disappearance and reappearance with the women.

"She lives," Lasan smoothed her hair back from her face, cupping the shimmering liquid in his hand and dribbling it over the wound just inside her hairline.

She moaned, her head turning away from him as the liquid adhered to the ragged cut, sealing it closed, then working to repair the damage that had been wrought.

"Garron destroyed the assailants." Queen Amoria rose to her feet and paced to the far edge of the grotto. "There was nothing left to question."

"Dragons have never been known for their even tempers." Lasan shrugged off the problem. There would be others to question soon. The Sentinel guards were capable of melding with the most evil minds to ferret out the information needed. They would find any betrayers who still lingered within the castle. Then, Lasan and Drago both swore, they would pay for their deceptions.

"They killed my man, the father of my children." The Queen's voice had Lasan watching her carefully, compassionately. "I have tried to warn my people that we did not defeat them all those years ago. But they have continued to believe our weakening power would protect us."

Regret and concern filled her voice.

"Queen Amoria, all of Sentmar is weakening in power," Lasan told her fiercely. "We have warned you of this. The magick rings around our moons should have warned you decades ago. This continued separation risks us all."

He was aware of the princesses aligning themselves with their mother, standing calm and silent, an obvious presence should she need them.

"I would have preferred that it be Brianna's choice to be a Consort of love. Not forced to be a Consort of power," she said bleakly. "I have the old writings, Wizards. The proof that both Cauldaran and Covenani began to consort for reasons of power rather than love. That they did not heed the laws of Joining, and they did not bring affection, nor respect into their homes."

She turned back to him, her brows lowered over dark worried eyes. "I would have wished more than that for my daughter."

"We have not even once deviated from the laws of Joining," Drago reminded her harshly. "From the moment we lowered ourselves before her, servants to her power, we have observed all things that the Sentinel Wizards and the Matriarch Sorceress demands. She is a part of us, Queen Amoria, heart and soul."

Amoria watched them, then her eyes moved to her daughter. Brianna was relaxed now within Drago's arms, not conscious yet, but breathing easier, a soft flush mounting her cheekbones, where as minutes before, her face had been deathly pale.

"Do you know, Wizard Twins, the other use the gods gave us the pools of power for?" she asked him quietly.

They inhaled roughly. They knew well the other use. They knew well that this would speed up the building power within Brianna, setting the Joining to come much sooner than they had intended. It would also build her arousal, her natural need and desire for them to levels that were once used as little more than excuses for royal orgies before the separation of the races.

"Queen Amoria, your daughter will always know our respect, and our caring," Drago promised her. "But to ensure this, it is likely a good idea that you and your daughters leave, so we may remove ourselves from its sensuous grip."

Brianna moaned, a soft, decidedly pleasurable sound as Lasan felt her moving against the burgeoning erection that strengthened between Drago's thighs. Lasan admitted his own erection was nearly at peak power now.

The princesses flushed in embarrassment, though Queen Amoria only rolled her eyes in exasperation.

"I will await you in her room." She motioned regally to her daughters and moved quickly to the arched stone doorway across the grotto.

"Grant me strength," Drago groaned then as his cock jerked against Brianna's tender buttocks. "Had I known this awaited me, I think I would have sat along the edge and merely dipped her in."

Lasan could not resist cupping her cheek gently and placing a tender kiss along the curve of her lips.

"Let us hurry," he groaned. "Before we both lose what little control we have and prove once and for all that our hunger is greater than our honor."

They moved quickly from the pool and wrapped Brianna's body quickly in a large towel before dressing and carrying her to her room. She was placed gently in her bed, left to the care of her mother and sisters.

As one, Drago and Lasan moved quickly to where the Sentinel guards awaited them. Someone had to have let the Seculars into the secured gardens. They could not have come over the walls, for the Snow Owls were nesting, and they had sent up no alert of intruders in that area, which meant a traitor resided within the castle itself.

Chapter Ten

๛

There was no sign of betrayers within or without the castle. Confusion reigned after the attack on Brianna, and no amount of searching, or scanning of the humans' minds by the Sentinel guards turned up any evidence. Knowing now that she was a target of the Seculars only increased Drago and Lasan's determination to convince her to agree to the Joining. The peak in her power could come at any time. The small amount of time she had spent within the liquid silver pools was already showing its effect.

That evening, Lasan followed her slowly as she returned to the gardens, though she did not venture too deeply this time. She stood beneath a low, overhanging tree and stared at the darkened area where she had been attacked.

Dressed in a long gown the color of sunrise, she was like a shining beacon, a promise of passion and heat. Her long, red-gold hair caressed her hips, shimmered in the light of the moons, and tempted his touch as few other things ever had.

"You should be resting." He stepped carefully behind her, aware of Drago waiting, none too patiently, in the dark privacy of his room.

Their passions were heightened now as well, due to their time in the powerful liquid of the gods. Heat seared their loins, tormented them with their needs and the remembered feel of her body. Impatience was edging their emotions to the point that even Lasan was beginning to feel the pressure.

"I have rested enough." Elegant shoulders lifted in a negligent shrug. "I am tired of resting, and I am tired of being hovered over. So do not hover over me, Lasan."

She did not turn back to look at him. Her voice was controlled, her tone even, but he could hear the rising confusion and imbalance that filled her. Her power was rising.

He stepped to her, laying his hands against the warmth of her shoulders and feeling the small tremble of reaction that rippled over her body.

"Brianna," he whispered, turning her to him.

Lust slammed into his loins, causing his cock, already hardened in need, to throb painfully. Her face was flushed, her violet eyes dark with arousal. Her breasts were swollen and rising and falling rapidly, the nipples hard, distended and pressing pleadingly against the cloth of her gown.

She licked her lips and he wanted to groan.

"Do you have any idea," he said roughly, "how much we need you?"

"Gods, there you go with that 'we'," she flared furiously, staring at him as though he had somehow mortally offended her. "I do not want a 'we', Lasan. What about you? What do you want? What does Drago want that you don't?"

Her defiance stroked fires Lasan once thought only Drago had.

She would tempt the patience of a Wizard Sentinel, Drago cursed.

A Wizard Sentinel was the most powerful, the most revered of the ancients. Lasan clenched his jaw as he silently agreed with his brother. His body burned for her, his heart ached to see her within his castle, stretched upon the bed that had been specially made for her to share with them.

"Then I wish to touch you, Brianna," he soothed her, his hand feathering over her bare arm. "It has been over a year since you have allowed me to taste your sweet kiss."

She jerked in remembrance and Lasan's body hardened. His mouth on hers, his hands holding her near as Drago's lips had feathered over her shoulders, her neck. She had been wild with need, her hips pressing against him, the plump mound of her cunt grinding hesitantly against his erection. His head lowered as he remembered her kiss, how her tongue had so shyly tangled with his. His lips met hers and he groaned out his need as she opened to him, seemingly as powerless in the grip of their lust as was he.

Desire wrapped around him. His, Drago's, Brianna's. It was a heat like nothing he had known in his life, a hunger that nearly stripped his control as he jerked her tighter against him, his hands dragging her gown up her slender legs, until he could caress the smooth satin of her thighs.

"Lasan," she cried out his name as his hand curved around the hot, slick folds of her cunt. She was wet, her juices flowing along the delicate curls and leaving him hungry for the taste of her.

His finger tested the sweet, slick passage of her vagina. By the Sentinel's rod, she was tight. She gripped his finger with fire and creamy passion.

"Come to our room," he growled, his finger pressing scant inches into the wet, silken passage, his cock tightening, so hard now the ache was physical. "Please, Brianna, let us show you how much we need you."

She tensed within his arms, a strangled moan of rejection escaping her throat as she fought now to be free of his hold. Lasan released her, despite Drago's silent, protesting curse.

He watched her with narrowed eyes, feeling her heat, seeing the small, betraying quiver of need that rushed over her body.

"We?" She shook her head, backing quickly away from him. "No. No 'we'. You, Lasan. Just you."

He pushed his fingers impatiently through his hair.

"Brianna, there is no 'just' Lasan," he groaned impatiently, his body throbbing with need. "There never will be, especially not where you are concerned. We are connected, spiritually as well as mentally. You will be a Consort to both of us, you know this well."

"I will be nothing to you," she bit out heatedly. "Nor to that stubborn brother of yours. I grow tired of hearing this 'we' fall from your lips. Perhaps I need to hear, just once, something that only one of you desire alone."

"Brianna, you are being irrational," he bit out, fighting for patience in the face of her heated defiance.

He wanted to growl, which was something Drago was prone to, not him. He never growled. But this woman tested his resolve. His resolve, and his lusts.

"Fine, you want nothing for yourself," she frowned at him her slender brows drawing together in irritation. "What about Drago? Is there not one thing he would desire right now, that you do not?"

He clenched his teeth, fury washing over him. She wanted to push his patience? Then she would see that there was most definitely a limit to it. Especially now, when all he wanted to do was thrust his cock as deep and hard inside her tight cunt as he could get it.

"Drago wants to throw you on the grass and fuck the defiance from your body," he finally bit out. "I am beginning to agree with him. So it would appear that once again, our needs coincide."

Her eyes went wide with shock, or excitement. He wasn't certain of which until her hand cracked against his cheek. Lasan controlled his grin and frowned down at her fiercely instead when the implications of her action sank in.

"Oh, gods," she whispered, her face paling as she clutched the offending hand to her breast.

"You have struck a Wizard Twin." He fought to keep the amusement from his voice and inject it instead with a foreboding tone.

Satisfaction filled him. He had never thought it would be so easy. Had he believed it would be, then he would have let Drago inflame her temper months ago.

"It was your fault." She was breathing harshly, staring up at him worriedly. "You had no right to speak to me in such a way."

Of course he did not. He was the most patient of Wizards and should have contained his temper. But this opportunity to force the little vixen's hand was much too good to pass up.

"You had no right to strike me, Princess, no matter the provocation. The laws were created for a reason. You know this well." He had deserved the slap, he well admitted to this. But it was forbidden for any female to slap or attempt to attack a Wizard Twin, outside that of a Consort. He could use it to blackmail her into a touch, a kiss —

You will not let that sorceress off so easily, Drago scoffed. I will demand a meeting with the Queen now. We can use this to our advantage.

Drago's impatience beat at Lasan with wings of lust.

It could do more to harm our cause than it could to aid it, Lasan warned him as he watched Brianna's expression turn decidedly more worried.

How could our cause be harmed much further? Drago argued in disgust. *The little witch is determined to deny us. We have not much longer to wait before she enters the zenith of her powers. We cannot afford to delay now that she has given us this opportunity.*

Lasan sensed his brother leaving his room quickly and heading for the Queen's, his expression a mask of determination, fierce and resolved.

Drago would not be denied now. Lasan sighed heavily. He would have wished to have Brianna another way. He would have wished for her cooperation.

"What are you going to do?" she asked him faintly. He could see the fear in her eyes.

"I will not harm you, nor see you harmed," he sighed heavily, knowing Drago was now set on his goal. "But I alone did not feel the pain of your blow, Brianna. Drago too felt it. He is not as understanding as I."

He kept his voice gentle, reassuring, though he knew the soft tone did little to sway her fears. He could feel it pouring off her in waves, trembling through her body as she fought to control it.

"No." She clutched his arm, her nails biting into his skin as she stared up at him, her violet eyes wide and shimmering with tears. "Don't let him hurt me, Lasan. He will if you don't stop him."

Lasan frowned down at her, confused by the sudden terror washing over her.

"Brianna, Drago would never harm you." He shook his head, lifting his free arm until he could touch the tear that trickled down her cheek. "Why would you believe such a thing as this? He would no more harm you than would I."

She was breathing raggedly now, her violet eyes wide pools of nearing terror.

"Why do you lie to me?" she cried out, jerking away from him, trembling. "What is he doing? You know." Her eyes widened further. "He's going to Mother."

Lasan caught her around her slender waist as she started to rush past him.

"No," she cried out, fighting against his hold. "Please, Lasan, don't let him do it. I will do anything. Please."

Lasan stilled, he felt Drago stop just outside the Queen's chambers.

"What would you do, Bri?" Lasan asked her, his voice soft. "Would you agree to be our Consort? Willingly?"

He hated the little whimper of fear that came from her throat. Why did she fear the alliance so deeply? Lasan could make no sense of the impressions of foreboding that escaped her.

He felt Drago waiting. His brother, for all his impatience, was filled with the same confusion, the same need to understand her denial of her needs as well as theirs.

Maidenly fears? Drago wondered. Lasan didn't think so.

"I can't." Her own words were filled with inexpressible sorrow. "I will escape you, Lasan. You and Drago. No matter the cost. I will not agree to this alliance."

Chapter Eleven

🔊

It was no surprise to Brianna when the guards entered the gardens to escort her to her room with the message that her mother would call for her when she was needed. She looked back at Lasan, seeing his closed expression, his bright emerald green eyes and wanted to rage at him. He had promised she would not be harmed, but Brianna knew better. She knew what Drago and Lasan would do. They would demand the Joining now, and her mother would have no choice but to force Brianna into it.

The law was an old one. A strict one. Due to the passions and sometimes volatile natures of certain halves of Wizard Twins, it was forbidden for any female, other than their own Consorts, to strike any blow to them. A female, even a Sorceress, could be severely punished for such a crime. A public spanking was one of the older practices. Brianna knew her punishment, though. Lasan and Drago now had what they wanted. An excuse to push her mother into forcing her into the alliance with them.

As she was escorted through the long hall that led to her room, she saw Drago waiting, propped casually against the wall, his dark blue eyes brooding, filled with lust as he watched her. She felt her body trembling, a shudder working up her back, heat filling her stomach, pooling in her cunt. He affected her as easily as Lasan did, despite her fear of him.

As the door to her room opened, the guards stepped aside, allowing her and then Drago as well, to enter.

"I do not want him here." She turned on the guards, her fists clenching at their closed expressions. "This is still my room. I am still the daughter of your Queen. You will have him removed immediately."

They stepped back, the door closing firmly behind them as Brianna stared at the thick portal in surprise. Shock vibrated through her system. She was aware of Drago watching her silently, his big body much too close, much too dangerous.

They were taking her over. She could feel it, sense it in the deepest part of her soul. They would have their way, despite her hesitation.

"You have destroyed my life, Drago Veraga," she whispered painfully. "Even my own guards no longer heed my words, but yours instead."

He watched her broodingly, his blue eyes brilliant behind the partially lowered shield of the thick, black lashes. She could actually feel his lust. It shimmered on the air around him.

"You broke the law, not I," he reminded her, though she could have well done without the reminder.

"Such bold, strong Wizards are you and your brother," she sneered to keep her tears from falling. "What a grave offense I offered you. To dare to strike the mockery from his face in retaliation of his insult."

She wished she had a dagger. She had little else to lose and nothing to gain if she could find the courage to cut his heart from his chest. Her luck, only a cold stone was lodged there.

"You sound as though we would have you beheaded," Drago scoffed, his dark voice husky, filled with his lust despite the seriousness of the situation. "Did Lasan not tell you that you would come to no harm?"

"You intend to use this incident to force our Joining," she accused him. "Aye, I consider this worse than death, you black-hearted Wizard. Had I wished the alliance then I would have agreed when first you made the offer."

She turned on him in her fury. All she saw was the cold, hard glint in his blue eyes, the savage cast of his features. For all his resemblance to Lasan, he appeared cruel, like a dark demon come to steal her soul.

"I am sorry you see it as such," he said slowly, watching her carefully. "I would have you at least find a measure of happiness in the alliance."

"Happiness," she scoffed, blinking back the tears that would fall from her eyes. "What happiness could there be? Shared among men who know no love, no tenderness? Subjected to the touch of not just one, but two, who would see to the theft of my very pride and decency?"

Fear coursed through her body.

"Where do you come up with such asinine ideas, Brianna?" He had the nerve to laugh at her. "We are not demons, merely men. And it is not your pride and decency, my dear, that I have a need to possess."

Heat struck her body. It curled around her breasts, burrowed into her womb and struck her cunt with a force that left her nearly gasping. Why did he and Lasan affect her this way? Why had the gods so punished her?

She stood shaking, trembling as he approached her. He was much taller than she. His shoulders were broad, covered in the silken material of his shirt, which tucked into snug breeches. The broad length of his cock was clearly outlined beneath the material. It was thick and long, and the impression of it sent fear racing through her once again.

He stopped just shy of pressing against her heaving breasts. His hand raised, his fingers brushing over her bare shoulders. Energy crackled along her skin, making her weak in the wake of pleasure that flooded her system. His other hand gripped her waist, and slowly drew her with him as he backed gracefully to the edge of her bed.

"I do not wish this," she whispered faintly as he sat down on the end of her bed and drew her slowly between his spread thighs.

He was heat and steely hardness. His fingers gripped her arms, his thighs, powerful and heavily muscled, encased hers. He was breathing heavily, his eyes darkening, the thick black lashes shadowing them with a sultry effect.

"Your body says differently, Brianna." His hands ran up her arms, his eyes never straying from the hardened tips of her breasts.

Brianna felt the pervasive weakness that overcame her body each time Drago or Lasan touched her. It infuriated her. It terrified her. Never had she known such a reaction to a man, and she couldn't bear the thought that her body would betray her in such a manner with this one.

"Do not," she whispered as he leaned forward.

His lips hovered at her breast. His face was flushed, his lips heavy with sensuality.

"I would only taste you," he groaned. "Upon my oath, neither I nor Lasan will take you until our Joining night. But I must taste you, Brianna. I beg you to allow that much."

"I cannot," she cried out, but her breasts were heavy, her breathing so harsh that her tender nipples, covered by the thin material of her dress, suddenly raked his lips.

Her legs weakened. She would have fallen had he not caught her against him, his arms wrapping around her, pulling her to him as his head buried between the swollen mounds. He lifted her, pulling her thighs around him as she cried out in surprise, forcing them to encase his hard hips.

Her gown slid along her upper legs as he sat her upon his thighs.

His cock was wedged between her thighs now, pressing heatedly through his breeches to burn the soft lips of her cunt. Brianna's hands clenched his shoulders, her nails pressing deep as she fought to hold onto her sanity. Her vagina pulsed, spilling the slick warmth of her body over the heated length of his erection.

"What are you doing to me? You are bewitching me. You and Lasan will destroy me," she cried out, her head falling back as she felt his lips on her bare shoulder, then moving with a sensation of fire over her chest.

"I am pleasuring you," he denied her charge, his voice dark and throbbing with his sexuality. "I am showing you, Brianna, why we cannot allow you to deny this alliance. I will show you why we can no longer stay away from you."

The ties at her shoulders were released, allowing the fabric to spill to her waist as Brianna gasped out in mingled fear and sharp desire. Her swollen breasts were tipped with hard, pink nipples. The elongated erection of the tips mortified her, but seemed to fascinate Drago.

She shook with a fever of conflicting emotions as his head lowered to her. Then she was arching over the support of his arm at her back, her wail one of sharp, painful pleasure as his lips covered a needy nipple.

He was greedy, voracious in his hunger. He suckled at her with hard, deep pulls of his mouth, making lightning arc from her breast to her cunt as he pressed his cock harder against her. His tongue flayed the tender flesh, then curled around it, stroked it. Brianna cried out, her fingers going to the overly long strands of his black hair as she gripped his head, fighting for her sanity amidst a wash of sensations so intense she felt consumed by them.

She no longer had control of her own body. Her hips bucked against the length of his cock as it pressed into her clit. She rubbed against it, her thighs clenching at the pleasure ripping through her body.

"I could live the rest of my days and never know again such pleasure as your body brings me," Drago groaned as he dragged his lips away from her nipple, the arm at her back bringing her closer as his head raised to allow his lips to caress her cheek. "Feel how hard I am for you, Brianna. How much I need you."

"You will destroy me," she cried out, though her body now had a will of its own, and begged for more of the heated touches.

"We will pleasure you, Brianna," he tempted her. "It has been a millennia since the Covenani has allowed an alliance between our two races. They have had a thousand years in which to forget the pleasure their women found in the arms of our Wizards. A millennia of hopelessness and searching for our race. I will not allow it to be taken from Lasan and me as well."

Brianna trembled as his lips brushed hers, staring up at him in dazed fascination as heat seared her lips, making her shudder and reach for his kiss.

"I do not wish to be shared." She was frightened of the Joining. The vast unknown and rumors of pain and anguish terrified her.

"Your fears are unfounded, Brianna," he sighed against her lips. She gasped as he stroked his tongue over them with a slow, moist sweep. "We are two parts of a whole, Lasan and I. We will bring you nothing but pleasure."

He gave her no time to deny his claim. His tongue parted her lips and swept into the moist confines of her mouth in a strong, bold move. Brianna stiffened in shocked ecstasy. His kiss was hot, carnal, sweeping aside all thought as her nipples brushed the fine material of his shirt and he taught her a way of kissing she had never known.

He teased her tongue into mating with his, stroking it, tempting her to shyly imitate him until he taught her with gentle pulls of his mouth how to suck at the sensitive extension. She followed his lead, now mindless with the pleasure. One hand cupped her breast, his fingers tweaking at her nipple, rasping it, making her arch closer and beg for more.

"Enough," he suddenly groaned as he broke away from her. "I cannot take you now. It is not time, Brianna."

He stared down at her, his eyes glittering with lust as he held her hips and pressed his cock harder against her. Brianna felt her labia swell and moisture gush from her clenched vagina.

Brianna fought for breath. There seemed to not be enough air in the confines of the room as she struggled for her sanity.

"Why?" she whispered. "Why can you not take me now?"

His eyes flared at the thought.

"I cannot, Brianna, without Lasan present as well. Our first Joining must be together. You are the heart we have gone without all the years of our lives—"

Reality splashed over her like a rush of cold water.

"No." She shook her head desperately. "You must take me separately, Drago. I will not object to the Joining. I will enter into it peacefully if you will swear it to me. You will not take me together."

Fear was a demon inside her. It curled throughout her body, chilling the passion that had raged through it seconds before.

Drago stared at her in surprise.

"Is this the reason you have denied our claim these past three years?" he asked her harshly.

"You will harm me. You know you will," she bit out, fighting to remove herself from his arms. "Do you think I have not heard the rumors, that I do not know of the women you have torn asunder?"

He let her go, but Brianna saw the shock and the edge of anger that filled his expression. She hastily fixed her clothes, watching him warily as he stared at her.

"So rather than come to Lasan or me about your fears, you have instead listened to rumor?" he asked her carefully.

"The Covenani separated from your men because of the pain and torture of the mating. All Covenani know this," she bit out. "I have no desire to be a sacrifice to your unnatural desires."

His eyes narrowed and his body stiffened with his fury. Brianna knew her fears pushed her now, not her desires, but she had no control over the images of savagery and violence that she had heard of for years.

Drago watched her intently, his blue eyes darkening, his face cold, angry.

"You would tempt a man to violence, woman," he growled. "I would suspect it was not the Covenani who ended associations after all, but the Couldaran who grew tired of the irrational, cutting words that fell from the honeyed lips of the women of your race."

"See, already you threaten me with harm," she charged him heatedly. "You have no rights to me when you would take me with anger."

"Take you with anger?" he bit out furiously. "When my cock is slamming into that tight little pussy of yours, then you may accuse me of such, my little sorceress. Until then, I would suggest you keep your accusations and your silly female fears to yourself. You may well find what a fool you have been if you do not do just that."

He did̦n't give her time to speak in retaliation. He stomped to the door and slammed out of the room with such irate male dignity that Brianna would have laughed had she not been so angry.

Chapter Twelve

℘

As the door slammed closed behind Drago, Brianna stomped her foot furiously against the hard stone floor. She winced at the pain that shot into her ankle and snarled silently.

She could not control the anger, fears and desires welling inside her now. Each time they touched her, each kiss, each inferno of sensation only pushed her and the burgeoning surges of energy higher. The muscles of her vagina clenched tightly, reinforcing its greedy demand to be filled. The remembered feel of Lasan's finger pushing inside that heated recess inflamed her desires.

She was fevered. Torn between the conflicting desires of her body and her fears.

As she paced to the far end of her room, a scraping along the other wall had her turning in surprise. A hidden door wedged open, admitting her nurse, Elspeth. Brianna frowned at the old woman over bright eyes, her pale, wrinkled features and the tight, pinched line of her once smiling lips. How long had it been, she wondered, since she had seen Elspeth smile?

"What are you doing here?" Brianna pushed her fingers through her hair as she watched the woman in concern. "Mother said you weren't to return for a while, Elspeth."

Elspeth's lips tightened further, her eyes narrowing in anger.

"Queen Amoria fears my love for you, child," she said darkly. "She knows I would lead you from this darkness she is sending you to."

Brianna could only shake her head. As she watched the dark, fanatic look on her old friend's face, she wondered if her mother and sister were right. Had Elspeth somehow lost her sanity with the loss of her child?

"Elspeth, you should be home resting," she sighed sadly. So many changes, so much that she must now accustom herself to. "I think perhaps you are ill, dear. I would like to send the healer to you."

Elspeth's head jerked up, her eyes narrowing further as her face flushed with anger.

"Their lies are corroding your mind," she sneered as spittle dribbled along her chin.

Brianna stepped back from her, suddenly, unaccountably wary of the old woman.

"I believe no lies about you, Elspeth," she promised her gently as she gauged the distance to the door.

She needed to alert her mother of the nurse's visit, and the locks that must have been broken to the old tunnels. How had she made the mental link with Drago before, Brianna wondered, frowning. Could she do it with her mother as well?

"I see it in your eyes," Elspeth kept her voice low, though hatred roughened the once kind tone. "They have infected you, those Wizard demons. Stealing you from me as surely as they did my child. I promised you, precious, I would protect you from them, did I not? You should not have run from those I sent after you in the gardens. You should have given yourself to them, allowed the merciful release they would have granted you."

Shock, horror spread through her. Calculation gleamed in Elspeth's eyes, and knowledge. She knew the blow she had just aimed and struck at Brianna's heart.

Brianna felt her knees weakening as pain tore through her heart. This was not Elspeth, the beloved nurse who had rocked her after her father's death, the gentle friend who had guided her through her youth.

"You are Secular," she whispered, the pain so intense now she could barely breathe. "The same who killed my father, our friends through the years. You have joined them."

She could not believe it, and yet she had to. She could only shake her head, staring at the woman she had loved so dearly for so many years. Desperately, certain she could escape the aging woman, Brianna sprinted for the door as she called out to her guards. Then she screamed in terror. From the hidden passageway, several men jumped for her as others rushed into the room. Elspeth was crackling gleefully, the guards were rushing into the room only to meet the swords of her attackers.

Before she could see them fall, or call out in fear to Drago once again, a blinding pain filled her head, and a darkness of despair and unconsciousness flowed over her. Her last desperate thought was of Drago and Lasan, and her foolish denials. Denials that may well result in her death.

Chapter Thirteen

Drago was admitted entrance into Queens Amoria's receiving room the instant he stepped to the wide doors. He entered with a fierce frown, his gaze going to Lasan, who he knew shared his concerns.

"We were just discussing Brianna's fears, Drago," Lasan informed him. "It would seem such rumors have abounded for longer than any memories here can place."

Drago looked to the Queen, feeling his fury swell within him.

"Our woman is nearly hysterical with fear at the coming Joining," he bit out. "Why were we not informed of this?"

Queen Amoria took a deep breath. Drago could see her hesitation and concern.

"It was for this reason, King Veraga, that we did not force Brianna into this alliance you have pressured us for. Had it not been for Lasan's continued vows that Brianna would never be physically harmed, then I would not have allowed you anywhere near my youngest child."

The Queen's voice was soft, lyrical, but with an edge of steel running through it.

"The Covenani desperately need your power and your forces to halt the Seculars in their continued attack against us. But I would not sacrifice the love of my baby for any of you. I would have wished that we could have continued to allow this to be Brianna's decision."

"As I stated before," Lasan spoke up. "She disregarded the rules—"

"As though it would be upheld after the offense you dealt her," Princess Serena, her voice much like her mother's, broke in. "I have watched over my sister this whole night, and may I say now you have not dealt kindly with her. She is not a Couldaran Wizard's harlot to be treated so shabbily."

The Princess's pretty face was carved into lines of fury as she stared down at the Twins from her throne beside her mother.

"We have agreed to go along with this asinine plan of yours and Lasan's, only for the safety of my daughter and my country." Queen Amoria came slowly to her feet. "After Lasan's explanation of the Joining, then I will allow the forced alliance. But should my daughter ever, and I say ever," her voice broke, her fury surging forth, "seek asylum from the two of you, then I shall place her where neither of you will ever see, speak, or touch my child again."

Why were we not warned by the Wizard Sentinel of these females' extreme emotions? Drago asked his brother wearily. Such displays were becoming tiring.

Perhaps he feared frightening us off. Lasan was more amused, more tolerant of the displays.

"We agree to your terms, Your Highness." Lasan bowed low in respect and indeed, he greatly admired the woman's gentle love for all her children. It was extremely rare among royalty.

"Very well." Queen Amoria drew in a deep, fortifying breath and began to speak again. Her words were halted when two guards burst furiously through the doors.

"Your Highness, Princess Brianna has been taken," the youngest cried out in fear, blood oozing from a gash at his forehead.

"Taken? How?" Queen Amoria rushed from the throne towards him.

"Through the hidden passages, Highness. I fear she was taken by the Seculars. They were led by Princess Brianna's nurse, Elspeth. We could not stop them." Distressed and wounded, the soldier went to his knees.

"Darren," Drago called out to his master guard, indicating his need to know where Brianna had been taken.

Lasan immediately telepathed his need to the other Wizard Twins in attendance within the castle. His lips quirked into a savage snarl of satisfaction as tendrils of magick began to race along the huge fortress, invading every corridor, every hall and hidden passageway it contained.

"We found them." Lasan frowned. "A dozen males and an older female heading along the lower tunnels." He immediately ordered sorcerer warriors along the outside walls to set up an ambush.

"Let's go," Drago ordered those soldiers still in the receiving rooms with them.

They rushed from the room, giving little heed to the women who had drawn close together, using their own powers to detect and protect their own. This, Drago knew, was the reason why the Covenani so needed the Wizards back in their bloodline. Their numbers were dwindling, as was their strength. As for the Wizards, they were much fewer in number as well, and were finding their world bleak and lonely without females who understood the tremendous responsibility their powers held.

We have seven warriors converging on the exit they're heading for, a Sashtain Wizard Twin announced as they raced through the Palace, heading for a servant's exit in the kitchen. *They will come out just below the Palace walls, beneath a small rise. It's level with the beach.*

Drago and Lasan ran faster as they exited the kitchens, following the directions being received from Sentinel Guard to Wizard Twin. Fury surged through them both, speeding through the psychic lines that connected the brothers. Their passion and possessiveness for Brianna was all consuming. They would kill those who dared to take her from them.

They met the first warriors as they skated down the incline to the river's beach. Power surged between them and Drago knew when the sorcerers jumped back from them that their eyes glowed and sparkled with the imminent release of the violence surging through them. They could feel the power building, rising along nerve endings, surging through their veins. As one they moved into place along with several other Wizard pairs as they connected with the tendrils of power that now wrapped about Brianna. Covenani and Cauldaran power protected her, though the Seculars were as yet unaware of it.

"We should take steps to weaken her power now," they heard a male voice growl just inside the entrance. "Take her before she awakens. With her innocence gone, her power will drain and her ability to draw from the Wizards will be destroyed."

Fury surged through Drago and Lasan in cascading waves of power. The act of rape against a virgin Sorceress didn't destroy her powers. It effectively ensured that when her powers peaked, that she trusted no male enough, especially Twins, to allow the sexual bonding needed to open the female soul. Only in such a manner could the Sorceress attain her full powers.

"Aye, and get our dicks cut off in the process should we be caught," another bit out furiously. "We must get her across the river first. Then we will show the bitch who controls her."

Drago scanned the bank carefully. There, hidden within the shelter of a thick growth of reeds, a flatboat awaited the kidnappers. Lasan called to the water and the waves rocked the small boat, loosening it from its mooring and sending it drifting into the dangerous currents. None of the creatures would escape their wrath.

They waited, a line of six Wizards and a dozen Warrior Sorcerers, as the kidnappers exited the tunnel. Before the humans could turn back, a shield of magick was placed behind them, leaving them but one way to go.

They came to a shuddering stop. Drago and Lasan watched carefully as the leader drew his dagger and placed it on Brianna's throat as she lay unconscious in the arms of another.

"It is the demon Twins who would use her to destroy us," an aging female voice spoke with raspy hatred.

Drago turned his gaze on the woman, feeling the insanity, the mad blood lust that gripped her. This woman had cared for Brianna as a child and would now see her harmed. He would have no mercy on her now.

"Kill the bitch before he can use her. Take her power," the woman demanded of the one who held the blade to Brianna's pale throat.

Lasan watched the blade. His eyes centered on it, his power shifting to become the steel that would slice tender skin and the vulnerable artery. The kidnapper fought to press it closer, to do as he was bid, but the blade would not touch the tender skin. The villain's hand shook as he fought to knick her, to assure the Wizards of the threat he represented, but no matter the strength he placed behind the blade, it would not budge.

Assured that no harm would come to Brianna, Drago turned his attention to the woman, the nurse who had raised her, should have loved her. Power sizzled in the air around the old woman, wrapping around her as she screamed out in terror. Bright tendrils of magick fed through her mouth, her nose, the openings of her ears. They burrowed through her body, traveled to her heart. She began to shake with seizures, gurgled whimpers escaping her throat. Within seconds, Drago's hand reached out. His fist unclenched, directing the powerful order to the energy that possessed her.

The power of the internal explosion ripped through bone and muscle, opening the woman's chest as blood sprayed in an arc around her. It splattered on the males staring at her in disbelief, the stark, crimson stain of her sins branding them with sizzling power.

Frightened screams filled the area as feet that once obeyed the human's commands refused to run. The one who held Brianna was screaming the loudest as blue and green strands of electric energy raced around him, surrounded Brianna, then lifted her from his arms. He grasped for her, but his arms were suddenly too heavy to lift. Like weights, they dragged him to the sandy ground.

All around, brilliant arcs of energy began to build as Drago watched Brianna float to Lasan's arms. He choreographed each tendril, drew them together for maximum power and then gave the final order to punish those who would harm their Consort. They wrapped about the necks of the humans, constricting, tightening and finally cutting off the passage of air to the desperately struggling bodies. All but one fell to the ground, their deaths coming amid harsh, gurgled growls.

The single survivor watched in horror. He wasn't as old as the others and Drago had detected his confusion, his fear when he learned that Brianna would be harmed. The lad had thought the defiance of his elders would gain them the release of the shield that kept them from harvesting illegally in the forests and plains of the Covenani.

"Do you see these deaths?" Drago questioned him coldly as silence prevailed.

The youth nodded, tears washing over his face, as he was held immobile by the force of magick wrapped around him.

"The Covenani no longer stand alone. Through the joining of Wizard Twins to the royal house of Sellane, power is once again restored. You will tell your people and those who rise against us, that they no longer fight women. They will now deal with the Couldaran."

Drago's voice echoed with menacing, raw power. The youth quaked, frightened whimpers of fear issuing from his throat as he repeatedly nodded his head. The scent of terror wrapped around the young man, much as Drago knew it would have wrapped around Brianna when she was first taken.

"I should kill you as well for not informing the Couldaran of this attack," he bit out, still holding the male within bonds of magick. "You could have warned the Covenani and this would have been avoided."

"I did not know," he finally cried out. "I swear to you, Wizard, I did not know until we entered the castle. We were supposed to be here to steal food alone. Our families starve, my mother and sisters are ill. I wanted only the food."

Drago frowned.

"There are no rumors of starvation among the humans of your land. Indeed your farms are prosperous."

"And our prosperity is stolen as taxes by the Covenani," the boy sneered. "We have nothing."

"And this is an untruth." Princess Serena stepped from behind the soldiers who had sheltered her since her arrival at the beach.

Dressed in a most un-Princess-like ensemble of leather breeches and a flowing white shirt, her long, thick auburn hair falling to her hips in riotous curls.

"This is not an untruth," the youth sobbed, tears falling from his eyes, his body shaking with fear and fury. "My own family lost all they had stored for the months that winter's cold prevents growth. We will starve because of the Covenani's greed."

Serena turned to Drago. "We do not tax those of a country that is not ours to govern, and never would we take more than any one family could provide. Many of our own holdings are not even required to pay, for they have not the resources," she told him, anger ringing in her soft voice. "I will know who would take the food of these people and blame the Covenani for the crime."

Determination wrapped around her. She would indeed find out, Drago knew.

Gesturing to several warrior sorcerers, he indicated the conquered would-be villain.

"You will escort this one to his farm along with a wagonload of provisions to see his family through the winter. You will ensure you are not seen by the humans."

And learn what demon steals from the mouths of innocents, he finished the order telepathically.

Drago nodded with a tight movement as the warriors gripped the arm of the youth. The magick trapping him was released and he collapsed against the hold of the larger men.

"Let us go. Brianna will be frightened should she awaken amid the death in this place."

91

Chapter Fourteen

℞

When Brianna awoke she was lying in her own bed, Lasan on one side holding her hand gently, Drago on the other, rubbing her arm in an uncomfortable attempt to soothe her as she opened her eyes. For just a moment, the variances between the two men hit her. Lasan, with his careful tolerance, patience and tenderness hid the dominant, forceful side of his nature behind the easy smiles and smooth charm.

Drago, on the other hand, allowed his dominant nature to be seen by the world. Forceful and commanding on the outside, he was not nearly as comfortable with the softer emotions he kept carefully hidden.

His hand reached out to smooth her hair back from her brow. There was a tenderness, a comforting warmth she had not thought him capable of before. His blue eyes weren't glittering with passion or hunger. They were dark with concern, and a shadow of fear.

In that instant she remembered. She jerked, her eyes widening as she struggled to sit up. Her mother and Serena, as well as her other sister, Marina, approached the bed quickly.

"Elspeth," Brianna gasped out, her gaze flying to the hidden passageway door.

"It's all right, Brianna," Drago spoke with a remnant of anger. "She is here no longer. You are safe."

The memory of Elspeth's face, twisted in fury, her hazel eyes alive with hatred, was seared into her memory. It was her beloved nurse, Elspeth, who had knocked her out after declaring her a demon. A whore for Wizard Twins. Tears filled her eyes as she stared up at Drago.

"You killed her," she whispered, knowing it was true.

For a second, pain flashed in his gaze. It was then wiped away with the cold, shuttered look she was more used to.

"Elspeth was mad, Brianna," Serena spoke in defense of Drago. "She would have had you murdered rather than see you rescued."

"I know that," Brianna bit out, flashing her sister an irritated look. "I was not blaming him for her death. But I can regret it."

What had happened? Brianna wanted to scream out to the gods. She had loved Elspeth, had depended on her care as a child, her advice as an adult. What could have driven her beloved Ellie mad?

She pushed her fingers through her hair as she fought her tears. Nothing had been the same since Drago and Lasan's arrival. They had changed her life, taken over, made a mockery of her need for independence and free choice.

"Brianna?" Marina stepped forward, her step hesitant, her dark gray eyes brooding and somber. "Elspeth has not been the same for some time now. You just did not wish to see this."

Marina had always been so quiet. To have her step forward, especially in the presence of men, was a surprise.

"Different," Brianna amended. "Not mad. She was never mad."

"It is obvious she was," Brianna's mother said wearily. "Come, Serena. Marina. We will let Bri rest. It has been an eventful day for her."

Brianna watched as her sisters rose to leave.

"And what about these two?" she bit out, indicating the men who flanked her. "Will you not see to their departure as well?"

˙ Anger surged through her. She had no desire to have Drago and Lasan present for whatever emotions would consume her as she fought to accept Elspeth's death and her part in the kidnapping.

Queen Amoria's slight smile was gentle and resigned.

"Those two are yours now, Brianna. I have approved the alliance. Come tomorrow eve the Joining ceremony will be observed and you will be Consort to the Veraga Twins. I believe should you wish them to leave, then you will have to order them to do so yourself."

Brianna knew she shouldn't be shocked. She had known that her mother would approve the alliance rather than see her punished for striking Lasan. But she couldn't stop the hurt from surging inside her. No choice.

She pushed down the softening feelings she knew she held for them, and allowed her anger to reign. They thought to secure their means by forcing her, by taking her pride and her dignity. By the hand of the Matriarch Sorceress, she promised they would have no peace in it.

She watched her mother silently. She would not disgrace herself or her Queen by arguing with her now that the decision had been made. But she would be damned if she would let Drago and Lasan by so easily.

"I did not do this lightly, daughter," her mother assured her, her voice soft, sad.

"Never fear, Mother," Brianna whispered. "I know who I have to thank for this decision. I will resolve this matter myself."

It irked Brianna to no small amount to know that had she been given time to consider her own feelings and desires, than she would have agreed to the Joining. She was no child, and was well aware that had they been the monsters they were portrayed, they would have never shown the restraint they had in the past days. They tempted her. She desired them, and was honest enough to admit to herself that she was coming to care for them. But they had no right to force her. No right to run roughshod over her independence.

Brianna stayed silent as her mother and sisters left the room. Her fists were clenched as she braced them on the mattress, her jaw clenched tight to keep her screams of rage inside. When the door closed behind her family, she rose to her feet.

Her lips tightened as the Twins rose as well. She turned carefully to Drago.

"I am your Consort now?" she asked him with a tight smile.

"Nearly." He inclined his head in agreement, his expression wary.

"So I can no longer be punished for the crime of striking Lasan?" she asked him.

"You can no longer be punished," he agreed carefully.

"Drago—" Lasan's warning came too late.

Rather than the paltry slap she had delivered to Lasan's cheek, Brianna now let her fist fly instead. The impact jerked Drago's head to the side. When he turned back to her, his eyes blazed with fury.

"You perverted, disgraceful bastard!" she screamed, facing him with all the fury that raged inside her. "Are you so depraved that you cannot find a woman willing to surrender to your unnatural desires? That you must force one into them instead? Did I ask for your attentions? Did I beg for your touch?"

Her voice rose in volume. She ignored the flares of energy that snapped in his blue eyes now, making them glow dangerously. Wizard he may well be, but she was a Princess of the royal house of Sellane, and by the gods, he was in her house. He would not dare harm her now. And by the time the Joining was completed, she feared it would no longer matter.

"You temperamental, vindictive little spitfire," he ground out. "How dare you strike me, your soon to be mate. I am your master from this day forth."

"My master?" Her eyes widened in mocking amusement. "You will never master me, you aging excuse for a dragon's last meal. Think you that you can use your male magick to bring me to my knees?"

"Uh, Brianna," Lasan's amused voice broke in.

"Shut up!" Brianna bit out at the same time Drago snapped the order to his brother.

"Oh, I will see you on your knees, you little witch," he bit out. "On your knees and whimpering for me as I fuck that viperous mouth of yours. Perhaps sucking my cock will give you better things to do with that poisonous tongue."

Brianna flushed, but she wasn't to be outdone.

"Go ahead, if you think you're brave enough to survive the bite," she snarled.

His eyes widened.

"You wouldn't dare," he growled.

"Stick that overused cock in my mouth and see if I dare or not," she spit out at him, leaning in close, her head raised as she narrowed her eyes in warning. "You have achieved your aim of owning me, and by the gods you may destroy me with your desires, but I will not go alone. I will ensure you live a hell just as painful as my own."

Drago's brows snapped together. He stared at her for a long, brooding moment before turning his gaze to his brother.

"We have contracted a mad woman!" he yelled, throwing his hands up as he stalked to the door in fury. "Deal with that viperous bitch before I stuff a damned gag in her mouth. I will listen to her ignorance no longer. The Sentinel Wizard has cursed us with this match. Cursed us, I tell you."

The door slammed behind him. Filled with a sense of satisfaction, she then turned to Lasan. One down, one to go.

"Do not even try." He folded his arms across his broad chest, his eyes narrowing on her. "You forget my patience. And should you test it too far, I will not stalk from this room, I will paddle your tempting little ass for sure. You don't want me that close to your sweet little entrance yet, Brianna."

She was breathing hard, the blood pumping through her veins, fury swelling through her body as she faced him. She was overly warm, energized; she would fight him if she had to.

"When Drago cools down he will know the reason for your fury, just as I do." He smiled as she frowned at him. "The time of the Joining is near. Your body and your power is preparing for it, my little sorceress. In payment for your heated words to Drago, I will allow you to wait now, rather than explaining this ritual." He inclined his head, his green eyes still amused, his smile just short of gloating. "Good night to you, beloved."

He turned and walked casually, gracefully to the door. He had the last word. The last laugh. Brianna growled in rage as the door closed softly behind him, reinforcing his control and his determination. Damn them all.

* * * * *

"Well, he knows the perfect exit if nothing else." Garron appeared at her side, receiving a glare from her rather than the welcome she was certain he was expecting.

"Damned Wizards," she muttered turning from him.

Brianna paced to the window and stared out angrily, her arms crossed over her breasts as she considered royal murder.

"I am pleased to see you are well," he surprised her then with his quiet, somber voice. Garron's sarcasm was known throughout the castle, and never failed to show itself no matter the circumstances.

She turned back to him, confused by the edge of sadness in his voice. But black eyes stared at her from the sharp, scale lined face. His huge mouth was turned down, his brow appearing wrinkled.

"Yes, I am well." She nodded slowly. "What is wrong with you? Are you ill?"

Through all the years he had tutored her and her sisters, Garron had never displayed such an attitude. He was sarcastic, mocking, a disciplinarian, a confidant. She had never seen him so saddened, though.

"I regret that I did not come to your aid," he said softly. "I could have saved you much grief had I not needed to leave."

Regret? There was a large measure of that emotion in Garron's voice. As Brianna considered him, she realized that other than one dark, bitter night in her and her sisters' lives, Garron had always been there when they needed him.

"You cannot be here at all times, I understand that, Garron," she sighed.

The great dragon had explained to her several times of the rest he often needed. Great magick required much rest after it was expended. Her rescue before and the effort need to carry others during the shadowtravel would have required great energy.

"These Wizards, they can protect you at all times, Brianna," he said quietly, the somberness of his tone remaining. "They would care for you during these times."

"Do not start, Garron," she bit out, frowning at him darkly, her hands clenching into fists as she propped them on her hips. "Those demons need no one else to speak for them. Try being on my side for a change."

His eyes narrowed, his lips thinned.

"Sorry, my dear," he snorted. "I always preferred the winning side if you don't mind."

Which pretty much summed it up, she thought. It helped her temper none at all.

Chapter Fifteen

℀

The Joining ceremony was scheduled despite Brianna's furious refusal to participate in or discuss the details.

"Brianna, I will have no more of this silence," her mother commanded her firmly. "I have told you repeatedly that the rumors are false. There will be no harm to you. And I know for a fact now that you have responded quite heatedly to their advances." Brianna had flushed in furious embarrassment that Drago and Lasan had dared to inform her of that. "This alliance is more than needed, as you well know. You will participate in the arrangements."

"I need no reassurances that I will not be harmed," Brianna sniffed angrily. "But I will refuse to participate in anything where I am not given a choice. As this matter seems to have been decided for me, so then can the arrangements for this farce of a Joining be decided as well."

Brianna agreed to whatever they suggested. No matter the suggestion her mother made, Brianna nodded her acceptance, until the Queen threw her hands up in exasperation and stalked from the room. She declared her youngest child possessed by the demons of stubbornness as she made her exit.

* * * * *

"You may as well settle down, Brianna," Serena told her later, her patient voice grating at Brianna's nerves. Her sister was too calm, too stately. Maybe if it were she getting ready to be the filling in a Wizard sandwich, then she would feel differently.

The thought of it made her heart race with building lust. The thought of the coming Joining filled her with fear, but not the fear of pain. She knew Lasan and Drago would not harm her now, but such intensity of emotion and need was just as frightening. She no longer understood herself, or the rising tension in her body. Like coils of sizzling heat tension wrapped about her body, inside her chest, making her heart race, her flesh so sensitive she could barely tolerate the air around her.

"I can't do this," she cried out, jumping to her feet as she paced the room. "Please, Serena." She turned to her sister, pleading. "Please, just help me escape. Let me out of this, in the name of the gods. I can't go through with it."

Serena frowned in concern as Brianna watched her. Fear raced through her, just as it had when they first touched her. They had stolen her mind. They would steal her soul as well. She was cursed. Cursed by demon Twins and their touch.

With a growl born of desperation, she turned from her sister and resumed her pacing. There had to be a way out of this. A way to escape Drago and Lasan. They could not just own her. She could not allow it.

"You are over-wrought, Brianna," Serena said worriedly. "Let me send for some tea and perhaps a snack before you begin preparing for the ceremony."

"Oh, gods," Brianna moaned as her stomach tightened at Serena's words. "What have I allowed to happen here?"

Power spilled through her in waves, as yet undeveloped, not yet centered. It glowed about her, making her tremble with this new awareness of her heritage.

"I have had enough of this," Serena bit out as she stalked to the door and threw it open. "I require Drago and Lasan immediately," she ordered the guards. "They will come to this room, or I will personally ensure that there will be no ceremony."

"What are you doing?" Brianna cried out in fear. "No. You cannot bring them here, Serena. You cannot do this to me."

Serena turned to her, frowning fiercely. "You will settle down, Brianna Sellane," she snapped. "You are a Princess, not a lowly born maiden to quake with virginal vapors. Control yourself this minute."

Brianna shook, fighting her tears. She couldn't understand her body, or the snapping, electrically charged power that seemed to sizzle through her.

"They have done something to me," she whispered, wrapping her arms over her breasts as she turned from her sister. "I cannot control this, Serena, even for you."

Tears filled her eyes and fell down her cheeks despite her attempts to halt them. She did not want Drago and Lasan to see her so weak, so vulnerable. How was she to fight them when she needed to, when she could not even control herself?

"You will leave us," Lasan's voice spoke with a gentle cadence to her sister.

She felt them enter the room. Both of them. Their power was a tangible force that seemed to suck the very air from around them.

"No." She turned quickly to face them, her body shaking, her blood screaming through her body with the force of energy building inside her. "Serena. I beg of you."

Serena hesitated, looking back at her with a frown of indecision.

"She never pleads." Serena moved to go to her, but Lasan laid his hand on her arm to stop her.

"We know well what is going on, Princess. Your mother was informed when you called us to Brianna that the ceremony would be delayed until tomorrow. The Joining will commence now. It can be put off no longer."

Brianna froze at his words. Her eyes widened and a shudder of fear, of longing and heat, convulsed her body.

"She's too frightened," Serena protested as Lasan drew her to the door. "I do not agree with this."

Brianna was barely aware of the heated debate going on between Serena and Lasan. It was Drago who came to her, held her, his blue eyes glittering, almost glowing within his sun-darkened face. She took a hard breath, feeling her breasts swell, her nipples hardening alarmingly at the aroused look on his face.

She wanted to speak, but she couldn't. Instead, she shivered despite the growing heat of the once cool room. Finally, the sounds of her sister's protests silenced and the door closed behind her retreating form. She fought against the tightness in her chest as she was left alone with the two brothers.

"I do not want this." But she could feel her vagina preparing itself for them. Heating, melting, the thick syrup of her juices oozing from between her now bare cunt lips. The ritual of preparing her for the Joining had been rife with furious embarrassment. The denuding of her tender cunt had been accomplished through not just her furious barrage of insults, but also no small amount of blushing.

"Do you not, Brianna?" Drago asked her softly from behind, his hand smoothing her long curls back from her shoulder.

His presence was a warm, beckoning heat. She couldn't resist leaning into him, feeling his broad chest cushioning her weight.

"I need time," she whispered, trembling as Lasan stood before her, his fingers smoothing gently over her shoulder.

His perfect lips turned up into a smile of tenderness.

"Time has ceased to be a commodity we can give you, Brianna." His hand feathered the long strands of her silken hair as it fell over her breast. "Feel the power rushing through you. Drago and I have felt this all morn. It calls to us because you are a part of us. Our Consort. Created for us."

"You did this." She shook her head in confusion. "You did something to me."

"We touched you. We have kissed you and tasted the passion of your body. As the one meant for us, it was only a matter of time before your body demanded its relief."

She leaned into him. She couldn't help it. Her body craved him; the energy flowing through her blood demanded his touch.

"You will not own me," she declared, though she moaned in rising need as Drago's lips feathered her shoulder from behind. "I will not allow it."

"No, Brianna," Lasan promised her as his shirt fell to the floor and his broad, dark chest beckoned her hands. "It is you, beloved, who will always own us."

Drago eased her into his arms, then lifted her gently against him. Her arms went around his shoulders as she buried her face in his neck. There was a measure of relief from being held against him, but not enough. Not yet. She whimpered with the erotic heat sizzling through her body as he bent to the bed, placing her in the middle, hovering over her as his lips caressed her cheek.

"There will be no pain," he promised her, his voice roughening with arousal. "But what is to come will be very unfamiliar and may seem frightening to you, Brianna. If

Menage A Magick

you will but hold onto us and trust us, then even that will ease."

The hem of her gown was raised. A warm, male hand touched her lower leg. Brianna jerked, recognizing Lasan's touch instantly.

"Oh, gods," she whispered. It felt good. So good. Like warm, heated relief where her skin sizzled with pulsating need. "You will hurt me for my tirade yesterday alone." She trembled at the thought of this.

"A tirade resulting from your needs. We are here for your pleasure alone, Brianna," Drago promised her. "You are our heart and our soul. Your pleasure and your happiness come above all things. Never would I punish you in pain for your words, nor your deeds."

His voice was a soothing counterpoint to the heated strokes of Lasan's hands along her leg. She gasped then as she felt the wash of his tongue over her knee. Drago's hands loosened the ties at her shoulders and gently the gown was removed. Brianna kept her eyes on him, fighting the need to cover her body, to hide from their aroused gazes.

"Brianna," Lasan's whispered sigh singed her body as he moved to her other side. His hand touched her along the way, leg, thigh, hip and finally rested just beneath her breasts.

"Look at me, Brianna." Drago gripped her chin, turning her face to him, his eyes locking with hers.

As her gaze was snared by the glittering depths of Drago's, she felt the first heated wash of Lasan's tongue on her nipple. She cried out, her body arching as heat seared the distended tip.

"Listen to me," Drago urged her. How was she supposed to listen while her body was going crazy, being lashed by a sensual fire threatening to consume her?

105

"Soon, within moments, the sexual power Lasan and I wield will be released. As we touch you, see to your pleasures, that power will see to the preparation of your body. It will ease your muscles, it will turn what would be painful into a pleasure never imagined." His voice throbbed with his need; her body throbbed with the demand to receive it. "Do not be frightened, Brianna. Let the magick and the pleasure consume you and all will be well."

His lips brushed hers, Lasan's mouth covered her nipple. Drago slid his tongue past her lips in a kiss of greedy hunger that she met with voracious desperation. She screamed into it as Lasan's mouth began to suckle her with hungry intensity. Sensations rioted over and through her body. Drago and Lasan held her to the mattress when she would have arched closer, their hands working over her body, heating her further.

Their touch wasn't hesitant and gave little concession to her innocence. Their lusts were volatile, hungry and hot, and inflamed Brianna's as she would have never thought possible.

"More now, beloved," Drago urged her as his lips traveled down her neck, moving heatedly to her breasts.

Lasan began to move as well. Following the center of her body, his lips and tongue ventured closer to her weeping cunt. She could feel her juices moving slowly from her vagina, coating her bare cunt lips and sliding along the crease to her ass.

"I cannot bear this," she cried out, her head tossing as Drago began to caress one nipple with his teeth and tongue, the other with his hard, hot fingers.

Lasan was between her thighs now, spreading her, moving ever closer to her cunt.

"Now," Drago groaned, moving back from her mere inches.

Where the strange vaporous strands of blue and green energy came from, she wasn't certain. But they were there, moving along her body as she watched in wide-eyed pleasure. They circled her breasts, and she felt a tight, heated suction that ran from her nipple to her womb.

"Watch," Drago growled when she would have closed her eyes.

Her eyes opened, following his gaze to where Lasan was lowered between her thighs. She watched his head dip, his tongue extend. His eyes locked on hers, green, brilliant to match the green bolts of energy slowly caressing the rest of her body.

"Oh, gods," she whimpered as his tongue touched her clit. It was swollen, pulsing, screaming out for relief.

Around and around it went. Not really touching the sensitive nubbin, but the pressure from the flesh around it was driving her crazy.

"Your taste pleases him, Brianna," Drago whispered at her ear. "Soft and sweet. Delicate."

She couldn't halt the trembling cry that breathed past her lips. Her body shook with pleasure. From her breasts to her toes she was flayed with the most amazing sensations.

Soft caresses resulted from the energy edging over her, whisper soft, the tiny trails alternately soothed and aroused as Lasan's tongue tortured and tormented her with fiery pleasure.

"Drago. Drago, please—" She tossed her head, turning to him, needing his kiss. Needing something, anything to ease the raging hunger consuming her.

Flickers of heated warmth began to travel around her body as the curling swirls of energy continued their journey. Like stroking fingers of sensual fire, they scoured over her flesh, making her arch, then whimper in rising passion.

Lasan's tongue flickered over her clit, causing her hips to jerk, her mouth to reach desperately for Drago, attacking the heaving muscles of his chest. He groaned, his hands tangling in her hair now as her tongue licked, tasted, her teeth raked. His body rose slowly, and she could do no more than follow the path the hands in her hair guided her on.

As her lips wandered desperately over the taut planes of his stomach, Lasan's mouth covered her aching clit and began a soft, seductive suckling that had her thighs tightening, the pleasure building to an unbearable level.

"Easy, Brianna." Drago's voice was rough as her cheek brushed the thick, steel hard length of his cock. "Listen to me now, Bri. I want you to open your mouth, beloved. Take me into your mouth and suck on my cock. As you do so, the energy stroking you so lovingly will prepare you further. Do this, Bri. Do this now." His voice became desperate as he moved back, aligned his cock with her lips and slowly pressed forward.

Brianna was aware instantly of two things simultaneously. The length and thickness of Drago's cock was more than she could have imagined. Her lips wrapped over it, her tongue stroked and Drago's harsh, male cry filled the room. Then the energy stroking her began to probe. Her eyes flared open, rising to stare up at the lover whose cock she stroked within her mouth. He watched her, his blue eyes nearly black now.

"It will prepare you, Brianna. Allow the energy to prepare you, beloved."

Lasan's tongue moved lower as the hands beneath her buttocks lifted her. It plunged heatedly into her vagina. At the same time, the energy stroked seductively through the crease of her ass, probing, tingling, warming the little hole closed so tightly to it.

"It cannot hurt you, Bri," he promised her darkly. "Give it leave to enter you, my love. Allow it to prepare you for my cock, Brianna. For soon I will breach that very channel in a pleasure that will consume us all."

Lasan's tongue plunged home again, the energy pressed, stroked, then slid heatedly into the tight passage of her anus. Brianna screamed in pleasure around the cock stroking past her lips. She would have fought a painful invasion, would have fought the fear and unfamiliarity of the entrance had it not seared her with sensations so extreme she had to fight for breath. It probed deep, stroked in counterpoint to Lasan's tongue, then began to stretch her passage, warming it, lashing it with agonizing pleasure.

"Yes, Bri," Drago cried out. "Yes, allow it to prepare you."

She didn't know where to move. To thrust harder against the tongue eating hungrily at her cunt or to try to move to force the curling energy to fill her more fully. She was being stretched, moistened, prepared. She could feel it, sense it.

"Now," Lasan bit out as he pulled back from her aching, dripping pussy. "I can wait no longer, Drago."

But Drago seemed beyond hearing. He was pushing his cock harder into her mouth, groaning with a passion that sounded closer to pain, urging her to suckle his erection harder, deeper, ever more. The pulsing flares of heat in her anus were growing firmer, the stretching sensation easing, pulsing, opening her further as Lasan rose between her thighs.

With a frustrated cry, Drago dragged his throbbing cock from her mouth, easing her down despite her desperate bid to enclose the erection with her lips once again. His mouth covered hers instead, his tongue driving deep as she felt the broad, hard head of Lasan's cock enter her aching cunt.

At first, she knew only the heat and hardness stretching her tender entrance, then her breath caught in her throat, her hands clenched at Drago's shoulders and she felt Lasan plunge forcefully past the small barrier of her virginity. There was only the slightest pain, then heat, a stretching fullness that had her gasping, the muscles of her cunt clenching, holding the invader tight, milking the hard flesh desperately as she felt an explosion of impending ecstasy begin to build in her body.

Her body shook in the grip of the lust filling her, quaking through her with the force of a thousand shock waves. She felt her own power build, washing over her body, easing her further, driving her needs higher.

"Now, Brianna," Drago cried out as he moved away from her. "Now, beloved, you see the pleasure and the power to come."

Brilliance glittered around them. Blue, green and a violet aura surrounded all their bodies as Drago helped lift her. Lasan kept his cock firmly implanted in her vagina, she was held close as Lasan lay back on the bed and drew her to his chest. His lips took hers immediately. His tongue plunged past her lips as he thrust his erection deeper, harder inside her. Her nails bit into his skin. Gods, how was she supposed to endure such pleasure?

Drago was behind her now. She felt his fingers glance the thick moisture that his energy had spread through her anus. She opened easily around his fingers. He groaned her name, moved closer. She felt the head of his cock inserting itself into the prepared entrance. Thick and hot, the broad head pressed against the rear entrance as fiery fingers of sensation tore through her body.

"Binding heart. Whispered soul," he called out to her. "Magick and strength, power and might. Heart to hearts, soul to souls. Bind forever, to create the whole."

Brianna screamed as his cock slid firmly, smoothly to the hilt up her ass. Lava-hot pleasure erupted through her body, magick flared from her, from them. Then they were moving in perfect accord. One out, one in, thrusting hard and deep as their moans filled the air.

Lasan held her close to his chest, his lips at her temple as his cock filled her, thrusting heavily inside her vagina.

"So tight," he groaned with aching gentleness. "Hot and tight, Brianna. Your body milks me, beloved, until I want nothing more than to fill you with my energy, my seed."

His words drove her higher, as did Drago's.

"Tight—"

"Hot—"

"Yes, beloved, take all of me—"

They drove her to the brink over and over again, and yet refused to allow her to tumble into that final chasm of agonized ecstasy. Their hands held her secure, their bodies covered her, surrounded her, their cocks, so thick and hot, filled her, stroking desperately inside vagina and anus until the rocketing sensations threatened to tear her asunder.

From deep within her Brianna felt the power of her explosion building. She broke away from Lasan's kiss, her head tossing as Drago bent over her, both cocks filling her, possessing her. She was stretched, filled, pleasured as she never thought possible. She gasped for breath as her clit began to tingle. Energy circled it, suckled it, much as Lasan had. She felt the same sensation at her nipples, heated warmth drawing on her, mimicking the flickers of a warm, moist tongue as Lasan and Drago fucked hard and deep inside her body.

She was pulsating pleasure. From head to toe, the bone tightening ecstasy began to fill her, pump harshly through her veins, shred past muscle and cell until the conflagration began to erupt.

She would die, but she would willingly step into Death's arms as her body began to jerk, explode, and showers of exquisite heated release began to erupt around her. Above her, Drago cried out her name. Below her, Lasan gripped her hips, pounded harder inside her gripping, tightening cunt, and began to cry out as well. She felt the fierce, hot ejaculation of their seed into her body.

The pulse and throb of their cocks and the climactic explosion of her own orgasm as it ripped through her, poured out not just her release, but her magick, just as Drago and Lasan's magick poured into her as well. The spine tingling orgasm of rich fluids and soul-deep energy was like nothing Brianna could have imagined existed. It heated the air with its power. Poured over them, into them, surging through their bodies like a tidal wave of epic proportions.

When it was over, Brianna collapsed against Lasan's heaving chest as Drago fell to their sides. Lasan turned, cradling her, wedging her against his brother as two more arms went around her. The filling in a Wizard sandwich, she thought wearily before exhaustion, mental and physical, drew her into a deep, satisfied sleep.

Chapter Sixteen

ഌ

Brianna awoke bathed in warmth from head to toe. She was tucked beneath the blankets of the bed, lying on her side, Lasan cushioning her back, Drago doing amazing things to her front. His lips feathered over her neck as her head fell back to the chest behind her. His rough, sexy growl of arousal fired her blood as quickly as the heat of his lips fired her flesh.

"Are you awake, Consort?" he asked her with an edge of sensual amusement a second before his mouth moved greedily to her breast.

"Were I not, then I soon would be," she panted, her hand going to his hair to hold him there as his tongue raked her sensitive nipple.

The blankets were pushed away from their bodies, but Brianna had no need to worry about the chill of the early morning air or lack of fire in the fireplace to warm her. Drago and Lasan carried their own heat. A heat that threatened to burn her beyond anything she could have imagined.

She moaned beseechingly as Drago lapped at her nipples, then suckled one into his mouth with lazy sensuality. He looked up at her, his black hair tousled and falling over his brow in a rakish manner. His blue eyes were bold, glowing with his arousal, lit with his devotion. Devotion she could feel sinking into her soul. She was right. They had stolen a part of her, but they had replaced it with a part of themselves.

"Do we pleasure you, Consort?" Lasan asked her lazily as he stirred behind her.

His hands stroked over her buttocks, then below with lazy purpose. As she held Drago tighter to her breast, crying out at the greedy suction of his mouth, she felt two fingers sink slowly into her heated cunt.

"Yes," she cried out, her breath rushing from her chest as lightning strokes of pleasure lashed at her vagina.

As his fingers fucked into her slow and easy, Lasan began to place sleepy kisses on her shoulder as he gently pushed her hair to the side. His lips moved with drowsy sensuality over her flesh until they met her neck. There his tongue licked, his mouth suckled lightly, and he created a firestorm inside her that had her crying out in need.

They were a sexual intoxicant to a woman's tender passions. Each stroke of their firm hands and determined lips only drove her higher. Their heated words and husky sighs stroked the lustful blaze inside her cunt into an inferno there was no hope of controlling. As she screamed out her need to them, Lasan lifted her leg and Drago's cock pressed against the moist lips of her inflamed cunt. He sank in with a groan. Brianna could do naught but cry out again as she felt the steely erection separate the muscles of her vagina, stretching her, filling her erotically as Lasan moved back, allowing Drago to lay her back on the bed.

"Put your legs around his hips," Lasan encouraged her as his lips moved to her nipple. "Clasp him, Brianna. Make him drive deeper inside you."

She did as he bid her, crying out as Drago's cock seemed to sink deeper, filling her further. Her hips jerked at the powerful, forceful thrusts inside her cunt. Her legs tightened around him, the muscles of her vagina clutching at him, tightening as he withdrew, parting in heated welcome with his return.

Lasan moved to his knees, moving closer to her, his cock engorged and needy as he turned her head to him. Her mouth opened hungrily, enclosing the bulging head in her mouth as his body jerked against her in pleasure. His cock was hard and hot, pushing in and out of her mouth as his heated words encouraged her in her pleasure.

Husky male groans accompanied her own cries as the impending explosion of her orgasm began to build in her cunt. She could feel the tightening of her muscles, the agonizing ache of pleasure that only seemed to grow. She was flayed by sensations so intense she could only tremble beneath the onslaught and still, it stayed just out of reach.

"Easy, Brianna," Drago groaned as he refused to allow her to crest that final wave. "In a moment, beloved."

His hips were driving harder against her now. His cock, hard and throbbing filled her, retreated, tortured and drove her higher with each thrust. Finally, his thrusts increased, the heat and hardness of his erection filling her faster, stronger, striking a nerve center deep inside her vagina that began to set off the explosion building inside her.

When it hit, Brianna swore she had died. She lost all breath as the wellspring of incredible sensations, fire and lightning, heat and wonder seared her womb. Her stomach, her breasts, her very soul ignited as her orgasm rushed over her, spilling through her body. It released in a stunning outburst of energy, creating a violet haze that immediately flowed to Drago and Lasan, wrapping around them, sinking into them.

Drago cried out as her cunt tightened further about his thrusting cock. His hips drove his erection deep, hard, then his body tightened as his own release rushed over him. Brianna saw then the wonder of mating with Wizard Twins. Not just Drago, but Lasan as well exploded in climax. The hot blasts of seed spurting in her vagina, her mouth, overwhelmed her, poured over her, fed the inferno of her own orgasm. A rush of blue and green energy poured from them as strongly as their seed erupted from their cocks. Within seconds, Brianna felt that energy pouring through her, sinking into her, fusing with the well of power she carried inside her spirit.

She screamed out at the intensity of her ecstasy. Her body bucked, her hands clutched at each man as her body, her very being became overwhelmed with such searing, lava heat that she could only give herself to it and rejoice in it.

The Wizard Twins were hers now and hers alone. No longer, Brianna knew, would she protest the alliance they had demanded and ultimately surrendered to themselves.

The aftermath was silent. As Drago dragged his weary body back to her side, Lasan collapsed as well in the bed beside her. The blankets were hastily pulled over their cooling bodies as they tucked Brianna carefully between them.

Perhaps we have tamed the little spitfire, Drago's thought was filled with satiated amusement. *We will merely keep her worn from pleasure and all will go well.*

Lasan opened his eyes to stare over Brianna's head at his brother's pleased expression. Why, he wondered, did he believe it would not be nearly as easy to tame their Consort? If indeed, there would be any taming done. From the evidence of their courtship of her, it would appear they were the ones in danger of being tamed.

You believe this? Lasan asked him carefully.

Aye. Drago stretched lazily and closed his eyes as a victorious smile shaped his lips. *You will see, Lasan. She will be as tame now as that cat you possessed as a child. Draped over one of us constantly, concerned only with our pleasure —* "

Drago slid slowly into sleep. Lasan sighed and stared down at the woman they held between them. Why did he believe it would not be nearly as easy as his brother had convinced himself?

Chapter Seventeen

෩

The Joining ceremony was performed that evening, and despite Brianna's frantic fears that all would not be ready in time, it went smoothly and with a beauty she would have never expected.

She stood between Drago and Lasan within the great hall of her mother's castle, silent and in awe before the Sentinel Priests and Matriarch Priestess. She had never seen such a unit before. Reclusive and more powerful than even Wizard Twins, the Sentinel Priests and Matriarch Priestess were the messengers of the gods.

The two priests stood tall and handsome, with long golden hair flowing to their shoulders, their eyes, one of gray, one of blue, watched her, Lasan and Drago with unmatched wisdom and fatherly affection. Between them, the priestess stood, gowned in rich amber and turquoise, her long black hair flowing to her hips.

No words were spoken, and the assembled guests stood in awe. None could remember a time when the Priests and Priestess had been seen.

"A millennia of separation has ended." The two priests spoke as one now as Drago, Lasan, and Brianna knelt before them. "The power of our Sentinel Wizards and our devoted Matriarch Sorceress flow forth, binding Wizard and Sorceress together, binding magick and devotion, wisdom and truth. " The Sentinel Priests and their Matriarch Priestess clasped hands.

They then created a circle as their free hand clasped the shoulder of Drago and Lasan.

"May the forces of our kind, our planet and our gods, return once again."

Brianna gasped, but could not move. Energy moved swiftly, searingly through Drago, herself, then Lasan. It enfolded them, wrapped them together, bound them. She would have whimpered had she the strength, would have stood in awe as she felt herself become a spiritual part of the two men who held her heart had she not lost herself to the rapture of it.

Arrogance, determination, devotion and fears, they all flowed through her. For a moment in time she was them and they were her. As the power built, then receded, Briana was left with a small measure of their force still warming her, comforting her. She knew they too would feel a part of her always residing within their souls as well.

And as the power of the priestly unit slowly drew away, she felt something more. A connection, a bonding to the very air around her. An intensity to the growing power inside that she knew she would delve more deeply into when time permitted.

"You may rise." The priests and priestess stepped back, watching them in approval before turning to the assembled guests. "In a thousand years our land has not known such a unit. Such a complete bonding of the land's powers and all it is. Meet the Select. No longer are they separate, no longer apart. Wizard Twins and Covenani Sorceress are once again, as one."

The Select. The words vibrated through her mind, her soul. They were, the Veraga Select.

As the celebration then commenced, the blue-eyed Sentinel Priest turned to her, a questioning expression on his face. "I have heard of the dragon who protects this land, Garron. I do not see him here to celebrate your Joining."

"Garron comes and goes at will, Your Grace," she told him with a slight smile. "He is a most stubborn dragon."

"Hm. Should you see this most stubborn dragon again, inform him the Taladen Select sends him their well wishes. He heeds our call no more than he does any others."

"I will be certain to give him your kind message," she said, bowing her head respectfully.

"Be at peace and in power, Veraga Select." The gray-eyed priest then said gently, "And know you are always welcome in the Temple of the Gods."

And they were gone. As suddenly as they had appeared, they dissolved, leaving Brianna with a sense of well being, and blessing.

"So Consort, perhaps your Joining was not as terrible as you feared?" Drago's hand touched her waist as he and Lasan turned her to the banquet tables.

"Don't get over-confident, Drago, it isn't becoming," she told him, though she couldn't halt the smile of happiness that crossed her face.

As they led her across the room, her eyes happened to stray to a twin set on the other side of the room. The Sashtain Twins, tall and nearly as blonde as the Sentinel Priests who had just graced the hall, stared with single-minded intensity at a lone female figure on the other side of the room. Brianna followed their gaze.

Her sister, Marina, with her long hair flowing down her back was listening in rapt attention to two small children eagerly displaying the gifts the Sentinel Priests had brought for them. There was a small doll, rounded and soft to the touch for the little girl, and a large likeness of the great Snow Owls with soft feathers covering their bodies and extended wings for the little boy.

Brianna frowned. Her gaze went back to the Sashtain Twins, re-followed their direction of attention and then returned.

"Lasan..." she began worriedly.

"Brianna." They stopped. Lasan looked down at her, his gaze warm, comforting. "Do you trust us now?"

She blinked up at him, and knew she did. Totally.

"Yes," she whispered.

"Then do not worry about your sisters or your people. The Sentinel Wizards are looking after us all. Just as they did our Joining. We must trust in them now, and what they have planned."

Brianna bit her lip, debating, wondering if she should reveal Marina's secret or keep it as her sister had pledged her to do so long ago. She glanced over at Marina, then back to the large Twins concentrating on her so heavily. Slowly she nodded. She would trust in them now, but she feared that the day would come, and soon, when that secret must be revealed.

Chapter Eighteen
Veraga Palace
Couldaran Territory
Two months later

ॐ

Pottery shattered to the sound of the bedroom door slamming. A furious female voice was raised in anger, echoing about the upper halls as Brianna, Consort to the Veraga Twins, vented her rapidly rising fury at the departing back of Drago Veraga.

"You dirty dragon dropping!" she screamed through the portal. "I'll be damned if I'll allow you to do this." Her furious outburst was accompanied by the sound of yet another shattered belonging.

Lasan rushed up the steps, knowing his Consort's fury was reaching a dangerous level. Much higher, and they would once again be sleeping in their separate, lonely rooms for only the Sentinel Wizards knew how long.

And he had no doubt the fault lay at Drago's feet. Lasan was becoming well accustomed to the fact that his twin was destined to keep their Consort infuriated with them. Which was all well and good, as long it didn't get them thrown out of the bed they shared with her.

"Can you not stay out of trouble?" he bit out as he met his brother just outside the room. "By the gods, Drago, I do not relish sleeping without our woman for another week, as you so obviously do."

"That woman is deranged," Drago growled, pushing his hands through his hair in extreme irritation. "She has lost what little senses she ever possessed. It was but a gods be damned request, not an order."

Anger throbbed in Drago's body, as it did in Lasan's. But where Drago's anger was centered on their Consort, Lasan's was centered on him.

"Just as tame as a little kitten, is she not, brother?" he sneered. "I will not join you in your punishment this time," he bit out as another enraged scream erupted from behind the door. "Does she not allow you in her bed, I will refuse to even consider requesting it of her.

He had done so the last time. He had spent a lonely week in his own bed cursing his stubborn twin and his own ignorance.

Adjusting to their Consort's volatile nature was not always easy. The conflicting energies, her own and theirs, made her quick to temper, but also quick to the sexual frenzy their bodies now demanded. It was also extremely agonizing when she punished them for Drago's dominance and often ill-timed orders.

"I merely asked," Drago bit out. "I made a simple request of the woman. That is all."

"And what did you ask?" Lasan narrowed his eyes at his brother's guilty look.

Drago shrugged. "The Sashtains are coming to dinner, as you know."

"And?" Lasan probed.

"And, they are bringing Lisette," Drago answered him, his expression hardening.

Horrified disbelief filled Lasan at this admittance.

"Nooo—" Lasan groaned beseechingly. "Tell me, Drago. Tell me you did not ask our Consort, the beloved mate of our hearts and souls to invite that woman to her home? Her table?"

Lasan was beside himself with worry now. Lisette was none other than the very woman Brianna had found in the bed Drago and Lasan had prepared for Brianna alone. Their first day home, secure in her happiness, her possession of their hearts, she had walked into her bedroom to find the blonde ex-mistress naked and waiting with several of the sexual toys that Drago and Lasan had bought for Brianna.

Drago had laughed at the sight. Brianna had not been amused. She seemed even less amused now.

"Kai'el and Caise are friends, nearly brothers," Drago bit out.

"Drago, you are—"

"Dragon droppings!" Brianna screamed as she flung the door open.

Lasan's heart dropped, shattered, and he felt Drago's do the same. She was crying. Large tears ran down her face heedlessly, her lips appeared swollen, her pretty pert nose reddened, her beautiful violet eyes nearly black with her pain.

"Look what you did," Lasan yelled at Drago, his fist connecting with his brother's shoulder at the sight. "She cries now because of your foolishness. I should kick your ass all over this palace." And well he was prepared to do just that. He would prefer to fight his brother than lose the warmth of his woman's body next to him at night.

"Me?" Drago yelled back in astonishment. "It was a gods be damned request."

"Brianna." Lasan held his arms out to her in a gesture of tenderness. "Come, beloved, do not cry. You will break my heart."

He tucked her against his chest, glaring at his brother.

"How could he ask this of me?" she sobbed. "She was in my bed, Lasan. Mine. I did not even get to spend one night in my beautiful Joining bed. She ruined it. Ruined it all."

Drago and Lasan winced. This was well true. The bed had been hauled from the palace within hours and set afire. Inside, their fire breathing Consort blasted them both and barred the merry ex-mistress from ever stepping foot on the grounds in this lifetime, and the next.

"Brianna, forgive me," Drago whispered, seeing that the attention his brother was getting would earn him a place in the bed that Drago may well not get to share. "I was wrong, beloved—"

"Do not even bother." She stepped away from Lasan, tossing her red hair back, her eyes blazing, her tears flowing. "I will hear none of your apologies and by the gods do you ever mention that woman's name to me again, I will see you de-manned most painfully."

And she could, too. Lasan and Drago winced.

"Stupid men," she growled, then gripped both their hands and pulled them quickly into the room.

The door slammed behind them. Before either man could blink, Brianna had drawn them to the bed and was on her knees on the mattress, freeing first Lasan, then Drago's hard cocks from their breeches. Lasan wanted to scream out his pleasure when her mouth wrapped around him. Sweet mercy, but her mouth was the most beautiful caress in all the worlds. Tight and moist and so damned hot. And she did not leave him after a few loving strokes as she often did when Drago was present.

"Do not fuck this up, Drago," Lasan groaned in ever increasing ecstasy. "For the love of the gods I will kill you myself if you speak." He had clearly anticipated Drago's coming plea to Brianna that she forgive him. There were times when his usually taciturn brother showed no good sense.

Then Lasan could think no more. He was distantly aware that Drago had moved behind Brianna to pleasure her, to fill her precious body with his straining erection. But Lasan was past caring. Her mouth was paradise. Her soft hands were strokes of fiery pleasure. The climax building in his scrotum would send him rocketing to the arms of the Sorceress Matriarch, where all Wizards longed to go.

He heard her moaning, knew Drago was pushing her to her own orgasm. Lasan's body tightened as her suckling strokes drew him closer. His balls tightened, his cock throbbed. He felt her scream of orgasm, then felt ecstasy's death enfold him as never before. His seed exploded from the tip of his cock, bathing her mouth in his rich semen as she swallowed greedily. Then she arched, screamed, her power exploding around them, mingling with theirs and fulfilling the ultimate promise of the Sentinel Wizard and the gods.

Chapter Nineteen

ຄ

The dinner went off smoothly. The Wizard Twins in attendance were captivated by Brianna's beauty, as Lasan and Drago had known they would be. Their Consort was gracious, and welcoming to all. Even the much hated Lisette. The blonde human female kept a wary distance from the Veraga Consort though, deeply concerned with the snapping violet flares of power that raged in Brianna's gaze when her attention was called to the blonde.

Lasan and Drago were uncomfortable with her presence, even though they were well aware of the need for it. There was a traitor in the hierarchy of the humans who lived and worked with Cauldaran territory, and that link had been traced to Lisette. They needed her for the moment. They were betraying the betrayer.

As they explained this to Brianna, she stilled, considering the information they gave her. It wasn't an easy decision, but agreed to allow the woman within the castle once again. And now, none could tell that their regal Queen was harboring visions of bloodthirsty vengeance, except Drago and Lasan.

The dark power behind the Seculars was gaining in strength, and the Sentinel Priests feared the magick of the land would not re-balance in time to vanquish the evil force intent on destroying the Wizard Twins. That a being of power and rage was behind this, there was no doubt. Finding the identity of that being, or twin beings, was becoming the problem.

Secular attacks were gaining in viciousness and number as the months went by. There were now six magick Units comprised of Wizard Twins and Covenani Sorceresses, but their combined powers had yet to build to a level to ensure protection. There were still two precious Units not yet matched. Which made this meeting more than important for a variety of reasons.

Hours after the dinner and subsequent socializing, the Sashtain Twins retired to their room with the crafty blonde traitor. Her cries could be heard throughout the castle as they vigorously fucked her to exhaustion before wrapping her in tendrils of magick to ensure she would not awaken nor leave their room without their knowledge. Only then did the true meeting commence.

Deep beneath the castle, situated in a room protected from all outside forces, Drago and Lasan met with the Units who had gathered. Brianna sat silently, her expression composed, but her eyes brilliant with worry as she listened to the proceedings.

"Princesses Serena and Marina, the chosen Consorts to the Sashtain and Veressi Twins, are nearing their peak of power now." The Unit of Grace that had resided over the Veraga Joining ceremony now stood before them in concern. "These two will be unmatched in power when their forces are aligned with the Twins the Sentinel Unit created them for. But the Seculars are aware of this as well."

Several attempts had been made on both Princesses already.

"Our forces guard the Princesses as best they can," Kai'el Sashtain spoke up, his dark voice worried despite his assurance. Kai'el was as tall as Drago and Lasan, but there the resemblance ended, despite the fact that they were blood cousins.

The Sashtain Twins were as blonde as the Priests were, with thick long hair falling to their broad shoulders. Their faces were sun bronzed, harsh, and lined with the battles they had fought over the recent years with the Seculars.

"We would guard them ourselves if they didn't run at every opportunity we were presented," Caise Sashtain spoke up in irritation, his light blue eyes filled with frustration.

All eyes turned to Brianna. She looked to her Consorts, and Lasan saw the sadness then in her eyes, a flicker of secrets.

"Brianna?" Lasan questioned her quietly.

She stood slowly to her feet, her hands clasped before her as all eyes turned to her then. Lasan and Drago's chests swelled with pride. She was temperamental, and gave their arrogance little or no respect. And though she would rage at them when she felt her feelings were being trampled, she stood by them, no matter the cause, when the need arose.

In the two months she had been Queen of all Cauldaran, she had ruled beside them with such grace that they often strutted with their pride.

"I fear if you are seeing Serena and Marina as Consorts, that the battles may be harder than you envision." Lasan watched as she drew in a deep, fortifying breath.

"Highness, I know I speak for the Varessi as well when I say the knowledge that they are our own is a part of us," Caise said quietly. "We can do nothing else but seek them out."

Brianna swallowed tightly, glancing to Drago and Lasan once again.

"If there are things we need to know, this is the time to tell us," he said gently. "It will go no further, and know that they care for your sisters as we care for you."

Gaining her trust was not always easy in regards to the sisters that she protected, despite the fact that she was the youngest child.

She looked to Caise and Kai'el in sympathy. "Marina's power may never peak. And if it does, you may not have the chance to complete the bonding with her, no matter your desire, or hers."

Drago watched the Sashtain Twins carefully.

"If this is about Lisette." Caise swallowed carefully. "This liaison will soon be over. We needed to know…"

"It is not about that viperous wench," she bit out with a snarl of bitterness towards the other woman.

She took a hard breath, then cast a silent, pleading look to the Priestess who watched her in sympathy.

"Then we must know what could stand between us and the bonding with our Consort," Kai'el said harshly. "This is not a matter we can debate, Highness."

"Kai'el." The Priestess raised her hand for silence. It descended immediately.

Drago and Lasan moved to each side of Brianna, a warm support should she need them.

"Several years ago, Marina was attacked." Silence, fury, now lay thick and heavy within the room. "Our Queen mother is unaware of this attack, because Serena and I swore to never tell during the first moments we found her. We have kept our vow, only because the subject so distresses her."

"I would know by who." Kai'el's hand lay on the hilt of his sword, a clear indication of his intentions.

"She did not know, and neither did we." She stared into his eyes, gathering her courage. "We know only that there were two, and that they were large. Marina remembers nothing else."

Her words sounded as a death knoll within the silence of the chamber.

"Serena cared for her during that night and the next days," Brianna continued. "She would not allow me to do so. I covered for them with Mother, though now I deeply regret that action. Neither have been the same since. Marina hides from all men, and Serena has vowed her Consort will be only a male she can defeat in strength as well as intelligence."

Two women, needed, desired, and essential to re-balance the powers of Sentmar. One damaged emotionally, the other scarred to the very depths of her female soul.

"Serena will choose differently." The Veressi Twins stood to their feet, tall and aristocratic, their handsome faces reflecting their assurity. "We leave this night, Sire." His gaze went to Drago and Lasan. "With such information, we cannot leave the protection of the Princess Serena to others. We must begin our campaign before the peak of power begins."

"Highness," Kai'el's voice was soft, yet filled with fury and pain. "Marina will be well cared for. I promise you this. But she must choose the bonding. There is no other way. Not for us, or for our world."

"I wish you both, Sashtain and Veressi, luck with my sisters," she told them softly. "But I fear we may be facing bleak times. What was done to Marina cannot be undone. Whatever Marina shared with Serena, will never be wiped away. I see this in them at all times. I will pray though, to our Unit of Grace, that you can do such."

Only the Sentinel Wizards and Sorceress Matriarch, their gods, and their only hope, could clear these obstacles.

"Such will be done." Caise bit out, turning to Drago and Lasan as the Veressi had. "Come dawn, we will return Lisette to her home and head for the Covenan lands."

Drago nodded. "I will assign the Wizard Guards to keep close watch on her. Our prayers go with you, Caise and Kai'el."

The room slowly emptied, leaving Drago, Lasan and Brianna alone with the Unit of Grace.

"Queen Brianna." The Matriarch Priestess drew near to her, her hand reaching out to touch the Queen's damp cheek gently. "I cannot ease your fears, nor your worries in the coming days. I can ask only this of you. Trust in our Sentinel Unit, the Wizard Sentinels and our Matriarch Sorceress knows all. Her pain, her rage, they move to heal her, as well as our land."

"I will trust in this, my Lady," Brianna promised, her head lowering in deference to the priestess.

"And always remember, we are here for you, should you or your Wizards have need," the priestess promised. "Call on us, Brianna, for this is why we were created. We are at your service."

The priestess drew back then, a gentle smile shaping her lips as she watched the sorrowful Queen compassionately.

"Thank you, Your Grace," Lasan and Drago bowed to her kindness. "As always, we are at your service."

The Unit disappeared, just as they had the day of the Joining ceremony, leaving Lasan and Drago to comfort their Consort. They eased her tears, and her fears, and they worried with her. For now, it was not just their happiness at stake, but the happiness and security of all they had ever known or dreamed of having.

Epilogue

ଚଚ

Marina Sellane observed the small group of human males as they carted off the wagonload of food stores that they had taken from the small house by force. There were six of them; great hulking males whose cruelty had earned them her undying hatred.

Inside the small house she could hear the wails of the mother, but there was now silence from the daughter of the house. The father was yet lying in the dust of the yard. He breathed, but the bloody wound to his head would need attending.

Marina watched the wagon disappear around the bend in the road and rose hesitantly from her hidden position behind the thick, concealing foliage of a Peron bush. Its flaming red and blue tinted leaves had hidden her from the assailants to the home as she came upon it.

She arrived too late to help. But she had memorized the faces of those who had committed the crime. A crime on Covenani land this time. Her eyes narrowed in fury. Her mother would have each man in that wagon beheaded for this crime.

As she started to move around the bush, she was caught suddenly from behind. The smell of an unwashed body, the feel of brute strength had terror washing over her. Once again, memory and nightmare seared her brain. Two, so much larger, frightening, hurting.

Her heart was thundering in her chest, strangling her as she fought the hard hands holding her to the large male bodies. Not again, she prayed to the Unit of Grace. Please, in the name of mercy not again.

"What have we here?" a coarse voice laughed, and she heard the chuckles of several others.

Marina screamed out in fury. Her body bucked against the hold as her fingers formed claws and she fought to rake the hands holding her imprisoned. Within seconds another joined the first. Hard hands held her, laughing voices jeered at her struggles.

She kicked out at them, twisting furiously, desperately, but she could do nothing to keep them from stripping first her large shirt from her body and then her boots and pants.

"Hell, we have us a Sorceress. An unclaimed bitch to boot." Dirty, his face and hair matted with filth, the lumbering male laughed down at her furious face when he spied the birthmark that marred her thigh.

Marina trembled with terror. Her power was still dormant and she had few defenses against the men who now held her. Fighting to concentrate for strength, she sent out a mental call for help. It would be her only chance. Perhaps if there were Covenani near, then they could reach her before the rape she knew the males intended. It had been all that had saved her before. But her sisters were not near this time. There was no one she could depend on to come to her aid.

"Queen Amoria will see you put to death for your crimes here," she screamed out as cruel fingers pinched her nipples and another pulled at the small curls that covered her cunt.

"She'll have to catch us first, bitch," the bearded one sneered. "But you can bet you won't be the one to tell. The three of us will fuck the life out of you before we ever leave here."

"No!" Her scream was torn from her as two of them pushed her to the ground, holding her there as the third began to release his breeches.

She struggled desperately against their hold as she fought for the power to increase the range of her call. Gods, someone had to hear her soon. Surely there was someone near.

She was so intent on a psychic scream for help that at first she was unaware that the sudden screaming around her was not her own cries for help. As she tore herself from suddenly slack hands, she rolled to her feet, jerking her shirt from the ground with every intention of running to the forest for cover.

An agonized male scream behind her had her turning. There, locked in the swirls of gold and pale blue energy, the three humans writhed in fury and pain as they fought the paralyzing force of the magick containing them.

Breathing hard, stunned by shock, Marina fought to drag her shirt over her body. The buttons eluded her, though. She clutched the front closed, watching as two Wizard Twins strode casually from the forest line.

They were dressed in leather breeches and snug tunics, with dagger and sword strapped to their hips, though neither had been unsheathed. Their dark faces were brooding, savagely cast and arrogant. They watched her with narrowed eyes, rather than watching the humans they had ensnared with their magick.

"Princess Marina, are you unharmed?" Dark and sensual, the voice wrapped around her, making her breasts tingle, her womb to clench.

"I am unharmed." She nodded. "They are with those who attacked the family here and stole their stores of supplies. My mother will wish to question them." They appeared to be slowly suffocating from the force of magick enclosing them.

One of the Wizards glanced at the three. Heaving a sigh, he waved his hand. Immediately, bands of energy enclosed only the wrists and ankles of her attackers, holding them firm but allowing no escape. Then the Wizards both began a slow progression toward Marina.

Breathing hard, she watched the two warily. As they crossed her boots and breeches, the articles were lifted by an unseen force and placed within their hands. Their gazes were intense, heated. Marina's nipples hardened, her cunt heated. She didn't consider this a good thing. She backed up a step.

A small grin quirked their lips, heated arousal licked at their expressions.

"Come, Princess. Dress and we will talk." The articles were handed to her.

"Definitely, we will talk," the other sighed, his eyes going over her bare legs. "You had no business being here. Why are you not at the castle?"

Marina dressed quickly, or as quickly as her shaking hands would allow. She watched the Twins warily. They were the Sashtains, and seemed to be shadowing her every step. Sneaking out of the castle was becoming next to impossible. Leading her small force of Sorceresses in gaining the information she needed about the advancement of Seculars was growing harder by the day. Serena would be less than pleased by this development. And should her mother learn of her daughter's activities, then there would be no peace within the castle for years to come.

"I was visiting families on Covenani land." She finally shrugged as she buttoned her blouse and fought the fear that still held her breathless. "I did not expect to come upon Secular attackers."

Caise and Kai'el watched her broodingly. They were in no way fooled by her nervous smile.

As the male lying in the dirt groaned, their attention turned from her.

"I will call the Sentinel Guards and Sorceress troops to this place," Kai'el sighed. "You will return to the castle immediately, Princess, your mother would be most distressed by your activities this day."

Marina drew herself carefully erect.

"I do not obey orders of Wizard Twins," she bit out furiously. "There are two females in that home that require..."

"You have no place in that home," Caise growled, his golden eyes furious now. "You will return to the castle and allow the healers with your mother's troops to care for those women."

"This is not your call." But she backed away as Caise stepped forward, his face suddenly taut with his anger.

"Princess, you do not wish to test me on this matter," he growled.

Immediately, energy crackled in the air around her. Soft as velvet, yet strong as steel, coils of gold and pale blue energy circled the air around her.

"This magick is for your protection, and our assurance you do as ordered," Caise told her with a smug smile. "Return now, or I may have to check more deeply into this penchant you have to be where you should not venture."

"You have no right to order me. Neither of you do. This is Covenani land, not Cauldaran." Fury blazed inside her. Like a conflagration she had no power to control, it ripped through her body and mind.

"Do not test us on this, Princess," Kai'el turned to her, his pale blue eyes filled with desire, and something more. Something she refused to delve further into.

Immediately the power that circled her protectively became warmer, more caressing, gentle in its demeanor. Her eyes widened. Her sister Brianna had told her how the Verago Wizards used such power to prepare her for their heated love play.

"You will not." Fear, as deep and blinding as before tore through her. She could not imagine allowing such a touch, giving leave for the pain that she knew Brianna would surely lie to her about. Her sister was protective of her, she would never allow her to know the true depth of the sacrifice she had made for her people.

"Do as I said," Caise snapped. "Return now, Princess, before I lose my patience and show you what I do indeed dare to do."

For a brief second their eyes met. Power swirled inside her, blinding, intense. A surge of intensity she had never known, that terrified her to the soles of her feet. Before he could step closer, she ran for the woods and the large golden unicorn that had carried her through her forest. Escape was her only thought. That, and a terrible fear that she would never truly be free of the Sashtain Wizard Twins.

Enjoy An Excerpt From:

WHEN WIZARDS RULE

Copyright © LORA LEIGH, 2005.

഼

She crossed her arms over her breasts, staring back between the pair of them. "I am no toy to be tugged at, Sashtain."

Kai'el's amusement cleared as sober intensity overtook his gaze and he leaned forward in his chair, bracing his arms on his legs as Caise watched silently.

"You are wrong, my little warrioress," he growled. "It is no toy I see standing before me, but a woman grown and hiding behind her sword. And I, Princess Marina, am growing tired of lazing within this castle awaiting your consideration on this matter. Do not mistake my patience for foolishness."

The deepened tone was warning enough that this situation was rapidly growing out of her control. She watched the two men warily, feeling the shadows of fear rising within her. They were two. One she could battle and defend herself against, two would overwhelm her small amount of magick as well as her defenses.

"Ahh Princess, what unfounded fear," Caise spoke then, the gentle chastisement in his tone making her chest clench in despair.

How she wished she could trust them. And it wasn't just her innate fear of their strength and their power that held her back. But her distrust of their motives. She could sense much more going on with the arrival of the Wizard Twins within Covenan than just a desire to find their natural Consorts. Much more.

"Who is to say my fears are unfounded?" she asked him then, swallowing against her regrets, against needs she did want to feel. "You do not know me, Caise. You are concerned only with your own needs, your own purpose. What of mine?"

She had no desire to leave the land she had accepted stewardship over. She was tied to Covenan, and to the power that fed it. To leave it would be to leave a part of her very essence behind her.

"And you know this how, Princess?" Kai'el's voice was soft, throbbing with a passion she did not have to sense, for the magick that filled it throbbed within his voice. "This is the first chance we have had to even speak of wants, needs, or purposes. And it was a time forced upon you, rather than one you willingly chose. Perhaps you should give thought to the fact that we have not forced the Rite of Reception, but have tried to give you that choice instead. Does that not leave us worthy of at least your smallest regard?"

How sincere he sounded. Marina stared back at him, feeling the hunger inside her to believe his words. No, he had not forced the Rite of Reception, nor had he demanded a petition to Courtship. They shadowed her every move, mocked her desire to run from their presence, and stole every opportunity presented to them to fill her time. But they had forced nothing. They had demanded nothing.

And oh, how they did fascinate her. All fears and wariness aside, she could admit to that.

"What would you have me do?" She spread her hands wide then, staring back at him the question plagued her. "If, and I say if with great prejudice, I were to be part of the Brigade, what would your reaction be? To go to my Queen Mother, demanding my confinement? Demanding I cease? And were I to give you leave to court me, who is to say you would accept my word when I declared your suit not to my liking? How, my good Twins, am I supposed to trust that which gives me no reason to trust?"

"Let us make a trade instead." Kai'el's expression cleared, becoming serene, calm. Despite that, she had the strangest feeling some trickery may soon be evolving.

"And what trade would you propose?" She was interested, despite her misgivings.

"Something we would desire, in exchange for something you would desire, if you were a warrior sorceress, that is."

"Kai'el," Caise's voice was suddenly warning, intriguing her further.

"Go on." She nodded sharply, her eyes narrowing as she watched Kai'el.

He did not glance in his brother's direction, despite the muted, resigned groan that came from him.

"You will choose one of us, now. On that bed..." He pointed to the bed. "You will lie with him willingly, fully clothed, and allow his touch."

Marina could feel the color leaching from her flesh.

"I am not asking for the sexual act, Marina," he said. "I am asking you allow touch. No more. Whatever touch you do not wish, you will simply say 'no', your wishes will be heeded. But you will allow touch."

"In exchange for?" She was trembling. She could feel the small tremors racing over her flesh, fear rising within her mind.

They were large men, strong, powerful men.

Kai'el smiled. A slow, disarming curve of his lips, filled with laughter, filled with a sense of pending excitement.

"Tomorrow, on the sun's rising, the Twin you did not choose this night to touch you, will take you to the air on his Snow Owl."

Marina's eyes widened. No Sorceress had ever flown. It was unheard of. The great Owls heeled only to the Wizard Twins. Even Brianna had not flown upon the great beasts, despite her Consortship with the Veraga Twins.

"She would allow it?" Marina whispered in awe. "You would not lie to me, surely? Were I to announce your words were false, Wizard, then no Sorceress in the land would so much as aid you were you bleeding in the streets. Playing me so falsely would not be to your best interests."

Kai'el grunted at her words. "The Snow Owls would gladly allow you to ride with one of us." He waved his hand negligently. "And we do not lie, Marina. I assure you of this now."

She glanced then to Caise. "You would fulfill this bargain as well?"

Surprise reflected in his golden eyes.

"Twins do make pacts separate of each other, Marina. Surely you have heard of this? I will fulfill his promise, just as he would fulfill any I would make."

She shrugged at the question.

"Who is to say what is true and what is false of the rumors we have heard in regards to the Wizard Twins. I merely wish to be certain."

Sweet Mother Sentinel. To ride on the back of the Snow Owl, to stare down at the land below, and know the freedom of the wind rushing over her. It was a dream, one that had followed her since she had first seen the great birds flying above the Snow Mountains. Pure white, graceful in their flight and majestic as they coursed the currents above. Even her griffons were not as graceful as those lovely owls.

But first, she would have to submit to the touch of at least one of them. She would have to choose.

"What of the one I do not choose?" She licked her dry lips as her nerves rioted. "What will he do?"

The tension in the air thickened. Magick sizzled just beneath the surface and hunger, deep and filled with lust, swirled around her.

"Watch," Kai'el whispered with sizzling heat. "Much pleasure can be gained in observing, Marina. More than you could ever imagine."

Why an electronic book?

We live in the Information Age—an exciting time in the history of human civilization, in which technology rules supreme and continues to progress in leaps and bounds every minute of every day. For a multitude of reasons, more and more avid literary fans are opting to purchase e-books instead of paper books. The question from those not yet initiated into the world of electronic reading is simply: *Why?*

1. *Price.* An electronic title at Ellora's Cave Publishing and Cerridwen Press runs anywhere from 40% to 75% less than the cover price of the exact same title in paperback format. Why? Basic mathematics and cost. It is less expensive to publish an e-book (no paper and printing, no warehousing and shipping) than it is to publish a paperback, so the savings are passed along to the consumer.

2. *Space.* Running out of room in your house for your books? That is one worry you will never have with electronic books. For a low one-time cost, you can purchase a handheld device specifically designed for e-reading. Many e-readers have large, convenient screens for viewing. Better yet, hundreds of titles can be stored within your new library—on a single microchip. There are a variety of e-readers from different manufacturers. You can also read e-books on your PC or laptop computer. (Please note that Ellora's Cave does not endorse any specific brands. You can check our websites at www.ellorascave.com or

www.cerridwenpress.com for information we make available to new consumers.)

3. *Mobility*. Because your new e-library consists of only a microchip within a small, easily transportable e-reader, your entire cache of books can be taken with you wherever you go.

4. *Personal Viewing Preferences.* Are the words you are currently reading too small? Too large? Too... ANNOYING? Paperback books cannot be modified according to personal preferences, but e-books can.

5. *Instant Gratification.* Is it the middle of the night and all the bookstores near you are closed? Are you tired of waiting days, sometimes weeks, for bookstores to ship the novels you bought? Ellora's Cave Publishing sells instantaneous downloads twenty-four hours a day, seven days a week, every day of the year. Our webstore is never closed. Our e-book delivery system is 100% automated, meaning your order is filled as soon as you pay for it.

Those are a few of the top reasons why electronic books are replacing paperbacks for many avid readers.

As always, Ellora's Cave and Cerridwen Press welcome your questions and comments. We invite you to email us at Comments@ellorascave.com or write to us directly at Ellora's Cave Publishing Inc., 1056 Home Avenue, Akron, OH 44310-3502.

THE
☥ ELLORA'S CAVE ☥
LIBRARY

Stay up to date with Ellora's Cave Titles in
Print with our Quarterly Catalog.

TO RECIEVE A CATALOG,
SEND AN EMAIL WITH YOUR NAME
AND MAILING ADDRESS TO:

CATALOG@ELLORASCAVE.COM
OR SEND A LETTER OR POSTCARD
WITH YOUR MAILING ADDRESS TO:

CATALOG REQUEST
C/O ELLORA'S CAVE PUBLISHING, INC.
1056 HOME AVENUE
AKRON, OHIO 44310-3502

MAKE EACH DAY MORE *EXCITING* WITH OUR

ELLORA'S
CAVEMEN
CALENDAR

WWW.ELLORASCAVE.COM

erridwen, the Celtic Goddess of wisdom, was the muse who brought inspiration to story-tellers and those in the creative arts. Cerridwen Press encompasses the best and most innovative stories in all genres of today's fiction. Visit our site and discover the newest titles by talented authors who still get inspired - much like the ancient storytellers did, once upon a time.

Cerridwen Press

www.cerridwenpress.com

2935009

Made in the USA